What the critics are saying…

Hot Rod Heaven is a fabulous story full of unexpected twists and an ending that you won't see coming. ~ *Susan Biliter EcataRomance Reviews*

Hot Rod Heaven is far and away Melanie Blazer's finest piece of work yet. This is a heartrending and gripping tale of love, loss and second chances; a positively masterful job of storytelling." ~ *Tammy for Love Romances*

5 Angel "Take a doomed love affair, a controlling fiancé from the grave, and hot cars and you get this engrossing story." ~ *Serena, Fallen Angel Reviews*

"*Hot Rod Heaven* is a skillfully woven, subtly tense read that had me racing through the pages (pun intended). For any readers who enjoy a bit of suspense and fabulous cars thrown in with their romance, grab this book now." ~ *Michelle Naumann, Just Erotic Romance Reviews*

D0885767

Melanie Blazer

Hot Rod Heaven

Ellora's Cave
Romantica Publishing

An Ellora's Cave Romantica Publication

www.ellorascave.com

Hot Rod Heaven

ISBN # 1419952331
ALL RIGHTS RESERVED.
Hot Rod Heaven Copyright© 2005 Melani Blazer
Edited by: Briana St. James
Cover art by: Syneca

Electronic book Publication: February, 2005
Trade paperback Publication: August, 2005

Excerpt from *Dante's Relic* Copyright © Melani Blazer, 2004

Warning:

The following material contains graphic sexual content meant for mature readers. *Hot Rod Heaven* has been rated *S-ensuou*s by a minimum of three independent reviewers.

Ellora's Cave Publishing offers three levels of Romantica™ reading entertainment: S (S-ensuous), E (E-rotic), and X (X-treme).

S-*ensuous* love scenes are explicit and leave nothing to the imagination.

E-*rotic* love scenes are explicit, leave nothing to the imagination, and are high in volume per the overall word count. In addition, some E-rated titles might contain fantasy material that some readers find objectionable, such as bondage, submission, same sex encounters, forced seductions, etc. E-rated titles are the most graphic titles we carry; it is common, for instance, for an author to use words such as "fucking", "cock", "pussy", etc., within their work of literature.

X-*treme* titles differ from E-rated titles only in plot premise and storyline execution. Unlike E-rated titles, stories designated with the letter X tend to contain controversial subject matter not for the faint of heart.

Also by Melani Blazer:

Dante's Relic
Legend of the Leopard

Hot Rod Heaven

Dedication

Steven: For your inspiration, for your love, and for your love of cars. May we find our own Hot Rod Heaven someday. Thank you and I love you.

Special thanks to Patrice, Jaci and my editor, Briana, for helping me believe in this story.

Chapter One

Brehann Williams sat up and clutched the front of her soaking wet nightshirt. The darkness of her bedroom reassured her that she was safe in her own house, her own bed. Not reliving the horror she'd gone through two years ago this week. Tonight, actually.

The date would explain why she'd dreamt about the wreckage of mangled steel and billowing steam. The sound she'd thought she'd heard was simply one of the tricks her mind had been playing on her lately — the noise of deep rumbling exhaust and the rhythmic thump of a healthy engine. She was already starting to question what was real and what was simply a product of her imagination.

"Enough." She scrubbed her hands over her face, hoping to erase those visions she could still see in her mind. She needed to get up, clear her mind.

After tossing her legs over the edge of the bed, she pulled her nightshirt over her head and threw it in the general direction of the hamper. Dammit. Even her hair was damp with sweat. And it was only a little past eleven. She'd only been in bed an hour.

It was going to be a long night.

She reached for the bedside light. Anxiety, the doctor had told her when she'd explained that from time to time she had these intense dreams that left her clothes wringing wet with sweat and her heart pounding. "Anxiety, my ass," she said as she slipped a fresh T-shirt over her head and yanked the pillowcase from the pillow.

Wait.

That was a car door. A real car door slamming shut. Not dreamed, not imagined.

She dropped the pillow and felt her way down the darkened hall toward the kitchen. Once there, she peeked through the slats in the blinds.

Of course she couldn't see anything. Forgot to put on the porch light—again. It was a weeknight. Her neighbors weren't the kind to come and go at this hour. But tonight, one of them had to be. But there were no headlights visible, and truthfully, most of the houses looked dark.

"Paranoid." Observation, not diagnosis. Normal reaction. After all, it was only the second anniversary of Luke's death. That night she hadn't been in this house, though. She'd defied his wishes and went with her girlfriends up to a cabin and stayed the weekend.

They'd fought before she'd left.

He'd taken off with angry tires screeching and burping up smoke.

She'd come back to help his mother make funeral arrangements.

The rap on the back door caused her to jump and let out a terrified scream. Instinctively, she wrapped her arms around her midsection and backed against the wall in the hallway. Who was it? Who could it possibly be?

The shades were pulled. No one could see her, but she couldn't see out. Take that back. She could try the peephole. What would that hurt? Just to be sure she wasn't imagining this whole thing. Carefully treading across the wood floor that tended to creak, she retraced her steps back toward the door.

Whoever was there knocked again. She hadn't imagined it. Her mind couldn't be that cruel.

She closed her eyes and tried to cringe away images of a twisted and burned body standing on the porch, finger pointed as it said, "You killed me. You did it."

"No," she mouthed. Letting her imagination be fueled by the darkness and the date was not good. Perhaps her neighbor had a problem. Burglars didn't knock.

The deep night was unforgiving. Not even a silhouette was visible through the peephole.

She'd have to flip on the porch light and acknowledge she'd heard him — her — whoever. Feeling even more sweat trickle down the groove in her back, she reached out for the switch.

Bree leaned into the door once again and peered through the tiny hole. Nothing. Empty. "Well, dammit." She'd taken so long, they'd probably given up.

Praying she wouldn't regret it later but determined to prove to herself she wasn't a chickenshit, she flipped the deadbolt and pulled open the heavy door.

A figure stood at the bottom of the steps on the far end of the porch. Male, she surmised quickly. He was turned half-away from her, his face hidden in shadows. All she could make out was his dark brown hair, slightly wavy at the bottom. His shadowy shape indicated he was average to tall, had thick shoulders.

"Hello?" she called through the screen. As if that was much protection. "You there. Is something wrong?"

"Brehann?"

The sound of the voice stole her breath. A sound from the past, its rough texture accented with the near whisper level. It made her skin tingle.

"Who are you?" she blurted, denying the recognition. Even her own voice seemed far away, its sound drowned out by the thundering of her heart. It couldn't be. Not now, not tonight.

But then he took a step toward her and his face was bathed in the yellow cast of light. Wide, almond-shaped eyes, slightly crooked nose. Strong, sculpted jaw with a scar mimicking a cleft right in the middle. There was no mistaking him.

She gasped.

"It's me. Bash." He shuffled his feet, but stayed at the edge of the porch. "I'm really sorry to bother you, being this late and all, but—" he hitched a thumb behind him, toward the road. "But my car died and well, I was hoping you had a flashlight and maybe a few tools so I can get it back running."

Bree swallowed. It had to be a dream, all of this. How freaking coincidental was it that Sebastian Bernecchi showed up on the anniversary of Luke's death? She never blamed Bash—she couldn't—but he was a sore reminder of the final argument that had ultimately sent her fiancé off in a fit of rage. From which he'd never returned.

The day's heat hadn't totally dissipated. On the thick, humid air she could smell racing fuel and the scent of oil and grease—more reminders of what life was like before...

Stop. It wasn't like that anymore and that was that. Bash needed her help and by God, she'd get him a damn flashlight, then try to bury her head under a pillow so she wasn't a zombie in the morning.

"Gimme a minute." Where *was* a flashlight? Not like she'd used one recently. Why couldn't she think? Because some of her brain cells *stayed* asleep, likely...that would explain why she opened the door to begin with.

Garage. That's where she'd seen one last.

Oh God.

"Sebastian?" she called through the screen. She couldn't see even his silhouette now. "Bash?"

"Yeah?" she heard. From the sound of his answer, he was almost halfway between the house and the garage already.

"I don't have a light but...ah hell, I think that portable lantern's just inside the garage door."

No response.

She opened the junk drawer and felt for the key ring that had the garage door key. Her stomach knotted at the idea of going out there and opening that door. Not that the garage in itself was a big deal. All her yard stuff was in there where Luke's precious hot rod used to sit. But she didn't often go in there at night.

"Gotta key?"

There he was, at her back door, hand on the latch. Damn, it was hard to swallow. Which puzzled her even more — instead of pure guilt, she was all...nervous around Bash. It was just Bash, not Luke's ghost or something. Sebastian, her buddy — Luke's best friend.

Her lover.

She held her eyes tightly closed as her fingers wrapped around the key. Last thing she needed to do was think about that...mistake. No. Not a mistake. Just the memory of it assured her it wasn't a mistake, but it shouldn't have happened. Even once.

"Here," she said, opening the door and passing over the key. Their fingers brushed. She looked up into his dark eyes.

It was impossible to gauge his reaction, the way the light above him cast shadows over his eyes. She could see the grin, though, gentle and…intimate. There was something different there, though. He looked down at the key and then back up at her.

He looked older. More mature—and it wasn't like he had wrinkles or anything. It was in his eyes, the slow smile rather than that boyish burst of laughter she'd often seen. But hell, the last two years had aged her beyond her wildest imagination. How could she even think he'd be unaffected?

"Glad you're still in the neighborhood. Didn't want to leave her just sitting on the side of the road."

She nodded at him and looked down to watch his fist close over the keys. Thick, calloused hands that boasted many more silvery scars than she'd remembered.

God, those fingers. She'd never forget them. Shivers raced up her back at the memory of his hesitant hands on her body. What she wouldn't…

The back door slammed, closing off that wicked memory and reminding her that he wasn't here for anything like that.

A hollowness in her chest replaced the jitters. *Wait. No.* He can't leave. Not yet. She had questions. Or rather, needed answers.

She pushed open the door and darted out into the darkness.

* * * * *

Sebastian fumbled with the key, but his mind wasn't on the light or finding his way through the moonless night to the door of the garage. His mind was seared with the image of Brehann in her barely long enough T-shirt and mussed hair. With her cheeks rosy from sleep and that throaty voice that had never failed to ignite his system, it'd taken everything he had not to push through that door and gather her into his arms.

But that wasn't what he needed to be thinking about. Sex had nothing to do with why he was back in town after two years.

Well, okay, maybe Bree *was* the reason he came back, but it wasn't about sex. It was about how he felt, leaving her without getting to say goodbye or to offer his assistance in what must have been hell for her. And because he couldn't live without her.

"Bash," she gasped, nearly running into him as he felt along the siding for the door. It was insane how dark it was. He hadn't seen her coming.

"What are you doing out here? I can get this."

"I—uh—it's dark and I wanted to help."

He gritted his teeth and turned away, grateful that she couldn't see him. His fingers were numb and calloused from years spent gripping and turning bolts and various other hot engine parts on diesel trains, and now shaking as they were, it was damn impossible to find the groove in the door handle where the key fit.

"Good. Get this." He felt for her hand and pressed the key into it. It wasn't supposed to be like this. What was wrong with the damn car anyway? It'd been fine when he'd pulled down the road—full electric, no hesitation.

Gas tank had been full. Then it'd just…cut off. Flat-out fucking died.

As if reading his mind, she said, "What do you think happened to your car?" With a faint click, the door opened and she hit the switch to ignite both indoor and outdoor lights.

The question went ignored as he stepped into the past. Shit. He let out a low whistle. It was as if nothing had been touched. Posters of girls in bikinis leaning over fine but faded pieces of horsepower still blazoned the walls. The toolbox still held the calendar that he'd gotten Luke for Christmas that year, forever frozen on the month he'd died.

Everything was dusty. He ran his hand over the vise and blew the residue off his fingers. Nothing had changed. Except Luke wasn't here.

Or his car.

"You sell it?" he said, inclining his head toward the bay where a beat-up old riding lawn mower sat. They'd spent hours—probably weeks of his life working on Luke's hot rod, turning it into one of the meanest, fastest muscle cars in the area. He didn't ever remember what the garage looked like without it, without any trace of it.

He hated the way she immediately hung her head. "Had to. I couldn't make it without the money it brought."

"Damn. Wished I'd have known." He pushed his hand through his hair and reached out to touch her arm. "I'm sorry I wasn't here, Bree."

She turned away, not lifting her head. "There's the light. I've never used it. Hopefully the battery's still good."

He followed her pointing finger and saw the lantern he and Luke had manufactured one night. That had been one helluva night. But there'd been a lot of those in their eight-year friendship. Lots of all-nighters and crazy creations.

"Let's hope," he said, hoping his voice was steady. He wanted out of this garage and its memories. He wanted away from the guilt.

After all, he'd killed his best friend.

* * * * *

The car, a 1955 Chevrolet Bel Air hardtop, sat stalled about three houses up from Bree's. Hauling tools back and forth was going to be a royal pain the ass.

With the still-dark lantern in hand, he pulled the garage door closed behind him. "I'll be right back with this."

She flipped on a flashlight. He hadn't seen her pick it up, but he'd not been paying attention. He'd been trying *not* to pay attention.

"I'm going with you. I can help."

Help him go crazy, maybe. "Get in the house."

"No."

Damn, he didn't remember her being this stubborn. If Luke had barked an order like that she'd have run. But he wasn't Luke, and he needed to stop thinking like that anyway.

"Listen," he said as he pushed the aim of the flashlight down to the ground. Did she have to blind him? "I'm going to see if I can't push the car a little closer, in case I need more tools or something. You're *not* going to help push. Don't even ask. I'll let you know if I need something. Honest."

The smooth skin of her legs looked like honey in the faint light. The hem of the shirt just barely touched the top of her thighs, and he'd gotten one too many glimpses at the practical yet somehow sexy-as-hell white cotton panties she wore. He forced his gaze back into her eyes. Lord, she probably didn't even realize what a picture she made.

"You push, I'll steer. And I can help. I was in the garage getting my fingernails broken and caked with grease as often as you were."

Yes, she was, and she wasn't any less of a distraction then. He knew Luke had been suspicious of them for over a year. In truth, there'd been nothing between them. Hell yeah, he'd thought she was attractive and sexy and had everything he wanted, but she was his best friend's girl. That made her his best friend by proxy. He treated her as such, and she back at him. Until...

"Good. That's settled then." She aimed the flashlight down the driveway. "Lead the way."

He groaned. See? Thoughts of her distracted him to no end. But if she was up to walking around in her pajamas, so be it. He'd just keep the lantern off and get her behind the wheel as soon as he could.

"Trade me. And stay close. I don't want you stepping on a nail or piece of glass."

"I'm fine." His body responded with way too much blood to the groin when he thought of the prospect of having to pick her up her up and carry her back into the house.

"Let's do it." He passed the modified lantern over and accepted the flashlight. He focused it up the driveway.

Neither of them spoke as they walked side by side through the gravel-littered drive and down the sidewalk, though he was careful to go slow. That had to be awful on her feet, yet she never muttered a protest. Until he heard a gasp and her nearly squealed exclamation.

"Whoa!"

"What?" He immediately shone the light on her feet. No blood. No sign that she was favoring her step. Looking up at her face, he realized it wasn't her feet at all that caused her to stop short.

"Gimme." The flashlight was tugged from his hand. "Where'd you get *that*?" The round yellowish beam glittered off the chrome of the front bumper and grill of his car.

He took the flashlight back and started walking. "Um, I've had my eye on it for a while. Just had the chance to pick it up. Right before I came back into town. It's practically brand new."

"Damn, Bash. I'm proud of you. '55 right? This is a sweet car. I know you always favored these."

He smiled. She remembered that? Bree was more than he recollected. It twisted something in his gut even now — watching her walk around his car, appraise the curves and run her fingers over the window lines. "This is just gorgeous. Talk about immaculate."

"Yeah, but it's not running. Not much good."

"Let's get it in my garage. C'mon." She opened the door and got in. "Does it have juice?" The lights flooded the street and subsequently blinded him. She extinguished them immediately. "Damn! Sorry!"

Bash picked up the lantern where she'd sat it down and stood beside the driver's door. The window was still down. "Now what?"

"This clutch is a killer. I need two feet to push it in. Of course, the seat would need to be moved forward for me to even think of driving it." She laughed.

God, to hear her laugh. To see her sit there in his car, her grin as brilliant as a kid on Christmas morning—it did something to his insides he thought would never happen again.

"It's nearly midnight, hon. Let's get this car someplace so I can get it started and let you get back to bed."

"Oh," she said, the smile fading. "Right."

Bash's shirt stuck to his back and sides, but the car finally came to rest at the bottom of Bree's driveway. No way was it going to make it up the gravel incline to her garage.

"That's good enough, Bree," he said, trying to sound less exhausted than he felt. "Gonna light this lantern and see what I can do from here. Thanks for your help."

"I'm not done helping, moron. I'm up now. Might as well do what I can."

There would be no arguing with her, he'd known that after a few minutes in her company. He liked that. That was new...improved, rather. The old Bree would have voiced her opinion, but cede to the command. "Leave it in neutral, then. Just set the emergency brake." He opened the passenger door and extracted the lantern and flashlight.

"Got it."

He popped the hood and shone the flashlight into the engine compartment. There was no bright red arrow pointing at the problem. Of course not. So he started at the lower corner and methodically traced his way around the firewall, using the visual cues to help him mentally answer— What the fuck would just make a car *stop* but still have electric power?

"What are you thinking?" Suddenly she was right *there*, her arm and shoulder less than an inch from his, her elbows propped above the radiator. "You did a good job, here, Bash. This is as clean as any show car I've seen."

"Uh. Thanks." Boy, wasn't he just into intelligent conversation tonight? After wanting so badly to see her again. "Sorry, it's just pissing me off that it'd just die. Battery's good. It's not out of gas—and it didn't sputter or miss or anything to give me the slightest hint."

She leaned over and searched the various engine components as he stood back to try to take it all in and force himself into rational thinking. He was a mechanic for chrissake. Diesel, but he worked on cars all the time. Bree was right when she called him a moron.

He was. All he could focus on was the way that white T-shirt rose up over those creamy thighs and how much he'd thought about her since that night. It seemed like yesterday. How could it be over two years ago? "Damn," he breathed.

"What?" She stood up, and the shirt covered the delicious curves once more. Her wide, blue eyes were all innocent. "Did you figure it out?"

"Oh, no. I wish." His face had to be beet red. "Hold this." He handed over the flashlight and set the lantern on the breather cover. "You stand here—lean over if you have to—look around for any loose...any loose anything—or fluid or, hell, you know. I'm gonna check the bottom side."

Bash took the flashlight back and got down onto his back and wedged himself under the car, best he could. The underside of the bumper scraped his chest and tiny rocks cut into his back, but he ignored that and focused on what he should see and what he wasn't seeing — the answer.

"Wait a minute."

He looked up, expecting to see her looking down at him from between the headers and the firewall, but she'd already straightened and was circling the front of the car.

She kicked his knee, nearly tripping. He heard her laugh at herself. Where was she going? He watched those perfectly arched feet as she rounded from the passenger side to the driver side and stood on tiptoe just behind the tire.

"Whatcha got?" he asked, sliding out carefully so as not to decapitate himself in his haste.

"Dammit. I can't reach it. But it looks like a black wire — like a spark plug wire — off here in the back."

"Spark plug wire?" The skin was gone off the top of his ear and his forearm had a nasty scrape from something sharp at the bottom of the radiator core support, but he was now as confused as he was eager to see what she had found.

Damn. He almost forgot all about one frustrating '55 Chevy in lieu of the sight of her, toes now dangling midair as she balanced on his fender.

"Yikes," she laughed, kicking to try to keep from sliding into the engine headfirst.

"I got you."

Bree nearly jumped from the touch to the back of the knees. "Maybe you should try to reach it." She squirmed, both from the surprising shocks the graze of his fingers caused to shoot throughout her body, and the guilt of being caught lying across his fender.

"Coil wire, dammit. I can't believe I missed it. Go for it. I can't reach it any better than you, besides, my jeans would scratch the fender. Unless you've pierced your belly button, I think you're safe."

The wire was *right there*. She wanted to help. Now that she was this close, it'd be anticlimactic to surrender her position. "I need three more inches, Bash. I can even see where this is supposed to go."

"Good." He cleared his throat. "Lean on in. I won't let you swan dive into the carburetor."

She laughed. Good ol' Bash. But focusing on the wire instead of the light pressure of his rough fingers on the base skin of her thighs was a bit tougher than she imagined. If she wasn't fixing his car, she'd be reading a hell of a lot more into it.

And the bad thing was that she wasn't upset about those thoughts.

First the car. Then she'd send him on his way and perhaps head back to bed with memories and see if she couldn't dream about him instead of— "Oh hell." Bree pushed herself even further under the hood and plugged that wire back in.

Her bare, slightly sweaty legs stuck to the cool metal of the car. But Bash's hands encircled her waist and lifted her up, rather than forcing her to slide back down. "There," she said, dusting off her shirt. She felt rather triumphant.

Until her hands came into contact with the top of her thighs. The realization was swift, silent and if she had her way, would be deadly.

Oh. My. God.

She was standing outside — on the road in front of her house, no less, in the middle of the night, with a man — so what that he was Bash, longtime friend and one-time lover — she was in her freaking underpants!

She swallowed the pure poison of embarrassment and backed out of the light, tugging down on her hemline. "I hope it starts."

With a half-sob, she raced up to the house.

Chapter Two

How? Bree shook her head. There was no answer to that. Other than it was now after midnight and whatever common sense she once had was still tucked under the patchwork quilt on her bed.

Sebastian must have figured she was... With a swallow she visualized again what she'd done. Did he think she was throwing herself at him? Teasing him? How could she *not* have remembered how she was dressed when she walked out that door?

It was Bash. Plain and simple. Seeing him — feeling his presence — had knocked every other thought out of her sleepy head.

She dropped into the antique rocking chair and pulled her knees up to her chest then groaned. Before she did something *else* stupid, like answer the door like that again, she needed clothes. There was a pair of sweats right next to the bed — for just such an occasion. How was it that she'd glossed over them the first time?

"Bree?" she heard Bash's voice from the hall.

She jerked the warm-up pants and securely tied the waist string. "Yeah." Why couldn't he just have gone on home? Why did he have to come in, didn't he get it?

Hell, no. Typical man. She darted out to find him at the edge of the kitchen, pacing.

"Bash, I am so sorry for..." She flitted her hand down on front of her body and shook her head. "I wasn't thinking. About me, anyway. Tonight's bad—you...here. I dunno."

She turned to the sink and started fiddling with the dishes she'd washed before going to bed.

"Hey, come here."

Her blood raced hot and her stomach knotted. Those exact words were what had started it all. Before... "I-I-I can't."

"C'mere." Strong fingers pressed into the tightness of her shoulders and melted away the minimal security shield.

"Don't," she whimpered, half-trying to pretend she wasn't affected. But, boy was she. His fingers were magic. Had always been. And here she was all vulnerable because her emotions were in chaos.

"Why'd you run?"

Her knees were practically knocking together. But that wouldn't keep her from bolting again, if she had the chance. She sighed, unable to even speak.

Bash chuckled. "So you didn't pick that outfit especially to get me all charged up?"

She clenched her teeth, but the whimper still slipped out. With his fingers turning her body into some kind of hot, gooey liquid, it was far too easy to imagine those hands doing their wonderful magic on other parts of her body.

"Guess that's a no." He released her shoulders, chilling her and making her wish she had the guts to turn around and plead for him to stay.

"C'mon, tell me it was a maybe. Showing off legs like that can't be a mistake."

She couldn't help it. This was Bash, probably embarrassed right along with her — or at least for her — and making jokes the way he did so naturally. She turned and leaned against the corner, crossed her arms over her chest and let her face relax into a slight smile. "Typical."

"What?" he asked, mock horror lifting his voice half an octave. Tapping his chest dramatically he asked, "Me? Typical? You wound my pride. I thought I was above average."

She said it before she realized what other meanings were possible. "You are."

His eyes, already a shade darker than midnight, deepened into liquid pools. Unchecked desire. The plain truth of it did nothing except already heighten her awareness.

Bash cleared his throat. "Well, anyway," he started, backing up and looking around. "The car's running. I need to get going. It's been a long day."

"Stay," she blurted the one word, just like that.

"What?"

As if she could say it again. Already she was trying to figure out how to get around it. "I mean, what if it happens again. I don't want to think of you stranded out there without — help. And…" She let her voice trail off. Yes, she was still thinking about what tonight was. Knowing Bash was on the road so late at night in a temperamental car. Well, she just never wanted to face news like she'd heard two years ago ever again. "I'll pull out the sofa — or you can have the spare room. Recheck the car in the morning before you leave."

She noticed he hesitated by the door. She shouldn't have mentioned the spare room. The very sight of that room had never failed to conjure up the memory of her sweaty naked legs entangled with Bash's. Or the way their fingers entwined against the pillow. Did she want to imagine him back in that bed?

Her very heart hung in the balance. Stupid as it was, she almost felt as if his answer would be a prelude of their future. *No begging*, she told it. Yet half her body already knew exactly what she was hoping, even if she wouldn't admit it.

"I don't—"

"Humor me. I'm devastated. Let me...uh, redeem myself." *Good one, Bree. You're begging.*

He laughed. "I shouldn't, really. I need to get home."

Shit. The tone of those words tied a giant rock around her heart and sunk it into the well of humility. "I'm sorry. I should have figured you'd have someone to go home to. Married?"

The wide-eyed look on his face was almost horror, eliciting a laugh from her.

"To quote you, I guess that means no."

"Hell, no, I'm not married. Not even dating. So get that worry out of your head."

Somehow that made her worry even more. What was a girl to do under these circumstances? If he wasn't willing to stay, he would have left. He was just testing her, to make sure he knew what she was asking—she wasn't a dummy about that.

But who would stay—Bash, her one-time lover? Bash, her late fiancé's best friend? Bash, *her* friend and confidant?

"That's a relief. I hate to have the neighbors circulating rumors that'd get back to a girlfriend or wife, you know."

In three steps he'd crossed the kitchen and had her face in his hand. "What are we doing?" His question had nothing to do with the conversation before. She knew exactly what he was asking.

She swallowed and lost herself in his eyes. "I have no clue. What do you want to do?"

A smile spread slowly across his face as he leaned in. "May I?"

His intentions were clear. And welcome. Blood roared in her ears and her heart threatened to beat right out of her chest. Trembling in anticipation and unable to speak, she licked her lips and nodded.

He caught her open mouth with his and crushed her with a drive that stole her breath and any inclination to fight. This was right, Bash's body pressed against hers, his heartbeat pounding against her chest at the same intensity of her own.

She wore no bra, and her nipples tightened at the first contact of his strong, hard chest pressed against her. She moaned into his mouth, unable to stop the reaction. She backed up until he pressed her right against the counter. The rough material of his jeans scraped against her stomach, the thin cotton of her shirt little barrier against these feelings she wasn't expecting.

His hands trailed down her bare arms, then back up again, almost tickling the nape of her neck. She closed her eyes and leaned her head back into his palms. She nearly died as his lips touched the underside of her chin, velvety tongue slowly burning a trail to her collarbone. If he wasn't holding her, she'd surely fall.

With strength she wasn't sure she had, she hoisted herself up on the counter, putting Bash closer to eye level. And, without realizing it until he stepped in and pressed against her, bringing his erection in contact with her now damp panties. The sweatpants meant little. She could feel him there, feel his heat, even the thump of his pulse.

He lowered one of his hands to her breast, cupping it through the material and lowering his mouth to find the peak. She clutched at the counter for balance, completely at his mercy. As he left one nipple and pressed his lips to the other, then pulled it into his mouth, fabric and all, she gasped and bucked up against him.

"I want you, Bree. I've never stopped wanting you."

The words sent shivers down her spine, but also reminded her that this wasn't a dream. There would be repercussions for acting on these emotions.

"Hold on," she gasped, pushing him back with a sudden surge of strength. Lord, he was intoxicating. She couldn't believe she'd actually come to her senses. Or lost her mind. Was she really telling him to stop? Yes, she was. And surely she'd regret it for the rest of her life. But she couldn't bury guilt with even *more* guilt. "It's too fast," she whispered, avoiding his eye contact.

Immediately he stepped out of her space and dropped his hands. His smile however said he was anything but sorry for that intrusion.

She wanted to call him back. Or at least reassure him that it wasn't that she didn't want him, because, Lord, she wanted him. It was just...not right. Bad timing. Something.

But it seemed he'd already decided what she'd meant by her hesitance. "Listen. Thanks again for your help and for letting me use your light and stuff."

Prelude to goodbye. No. Not yet. She hopped off the counter and crossed her arms over her still damp T-shirt. "If you won't just crash here, at least visit for a bit. I hardly think working on your car qualifies as catching up. Go turn the car off and come back in." Without waiting for his answer, she walked into the living room and turned on a couple of low lights.

She heard the motor die and the crickets resume their nightly serenade.

Bash walked in and sprawled against the corner of the couch as if he'd never disappeared from her life, or her house.

"Can I get you something to drink? Eat?"

"Sit down here. You don't need to be playing...hostess or whatever you call it. Relax."

She took a deep breath and perched on the edge of the chair. "So," she paused, bit her lower lip and wondered if she wanted to know the answer. "Where have you been the last two years?"

His feet slid off the coffee table and hit the wood floor solidly. "Chasing my tail." His crooked smile was endearing, but she sensed it wasn't all as playful as he made it sound.

"It led you back here?" What *had* brought him back into this area? There wasn't much here in the way of jobs. It seems like all the people she had gone to school with had fled to the bigger cities and suburbs to the south.

"Something did." He looked around the room.

While she waited for further explanation, she watched his face, trying to see if she could gauge his reaction to the changes she'd made in the house. Luke hadn't allowed her to decorate it the way she'd wanted. It'd always been so dark and dreary. Now it felt good to get up in the morning and let the sun shine in.

"I'm proud of you, Brehann. You've done good."

He struck a chord. "Thanks. For a while there, I think you were the only one who thought I could. I've missed you." Funny how just verbalizing that had tears springing to her eyes. *Damn*, had she missed him. Especially those first few months when she had no idea of direction and was tempted to just give up.

"You finish school?" Bash leaned forward and rested his forearms on his knees. "Tell me you didn't quit."

A grin pulled at her lips. "No. I didn't quit."

This was weird. Way weird. Despite the flare-up of heat in the kitchen, they had now digressed to the way they'd been years before, making light conversation while waiting for Luke to get home or change or shower or something. Funny how she'd always been very aware of how careful Bash had been even then to keep their conversations on a subject that was neither too personal nor too engaging. Of course, he'd known Luke longer — and was probably aware of his tendency to be possessive and, as she saw toward the end, controlling. Hindsight — always so clear.

"What do you do these days?" he continued before she had a chance to start quizzing him.

"Boring stuff — accounting and paperwork for the school system."

"And when school's out?" She noticed the glimmer in his eyes and held it wholly responsible for the chill that popped goose bumps on all her exposed skin.

"Not much. Keep house, watch TV, go out with my friends."

"Glad you have them," he said quickly.

Which clearly meant he remembered the hell she'd taken about having any friends outside Luke's little circle. "Yeah. Me, too. Glad of a lot of things, in fact."

"How are you, *really*?" His eyes met hers, their unspoken message taking the simple question deeper than the mere words.

She broke his gaze and stood up, pausing at one of her treasured houseplants—ironically, one she'd gotten from the funeral home—to pinch off a yellow leaf. "Is it wrong to say that things actually *are* good? I don't think I'd be where I am now if..." She let her voice trail off. She'd said *since Luke died* hundreds of times, but right now it seemed better left unspoken.

"I knew what you dealt with, Bree. I'd be disappointed to find things weren't better for you now. Luke loved you, I know he did, but he didn't understand that what he did—how he treated you—wasn't right."

"I can't help but think if I—"

"Brehann, get over it. It's over. He's dead. It was an accident. You're alive and you're happy and you're damn well entitled to it."

"It wasn't an accident. I killed him, Bash. I never told you. Never had the chance to. But he knew. He confronted me about...about...about us, and I couldn't lie. How can I live with that? How do I deserve to be happy, to feel the way you just...made me feel, when he died because of it?"

She expected a reaction. At the least, slumped shoulders, but she wouldn't have been surprised if he'd gotten up, called her a murderer and walked out. "Bash? Did you hear me? I just said I admitted to Luke that we—"

"I heard you. But that didn't kill him. *You* didn't kill him."

Tears had welled up in her eyes and began to flow freely down her cheeks. "I just keep thinking that if I hadn't insisted on going on that camping overnighter with Kelly, we wouldn't have fought. He wouldn't have accused me of going to see you and I wouldn't have frozen up. I know he knew then. I saw it in his eyes. I can still see it."

"Do you regret what happened between us?"

The lump in her throat was almost larger than she could swallow. What a weighted question, but one she'd asked herself for weeks, even months, after the fact. "Us? Do I regret…" Just the memory of the heat, the passion, the fulfillment that he'd given her stole her breath. She shook her head, not negatively, but unable to answer.

He got up and approached her, slowly, eyes burning into hers but plainly giving her time to bolt. "Shame we can't change the past. But we have the future."

Bree turned out of his arms. These mixed emotions confused her to no end. "Bash, I—you…you just got back. Tonight's—"

"Shh. Don't think about it, don't worry about it. I'm not in a hurry to leave again. But I want to be in your life."

How dare she hope? How dare she taint Luke's memory by continuing the affair that, regardless of what Bash insisted, had contributed to his death. She shook her head. "I don't know. I—"

"Go on to bed, Brehann. I'll lock up. You'll be safe. Even from me."

* * * * *

Bree heard him go outside. She tensed in fear that he was leaving when his car fired again, but then she heard the electric hum of the garage door opener and realized that he'd tucked that beautiful car inside. How symbolic was that?

She stared at the ceiling, the shadows cast by the faint light that filtered in through the edge of her blinds tweaking her imagination. Never ever could she have imagined seeing Sebastian like this. She'd seen him last early the afternoon when Luke had died.

Clear as watching a video, her mind replayed those fateful last hours.

Bash had pulled up. Luke was already in the garage, so there'd been no need for her to go out there. Luke had been drinking. And they'd argued again about her plans for the weekend. Kelly's sister and her husband had offered their fishing cabin up for a weekend getaway and a group of about five girls had planned this two-night trip for over a month.

She remembered being glad Bash had arrived. It'd be easier for her to escape if he were there.

Bree closed her eyes against the sound of his footsteps crunching on the gravel outside her window and then as he climbed the steps.

The memories flooded back faster, the details clearer now. She had confided in Bash the night before that she'd not only postponed the tentative wedding date she and Luke had set, but put it off indefinitely. In fact, she could hear her own voice saying to Bash, "I'm here for all the wrong reasons. My goal is to get things in order and leave, if only to make him see how he's driven me away."

But things hadn't worked out that way. Bash had only stayed a few minutes, waving to her as he'd pulled away in his beat up Jeep. She'd watched, cursing her bad luck and offering a wave that was supposed to say, *Thanks, pal, I was supposed to leave first.* She watched until his vehicle was out of sight.

Her attention to Bash didn't go unnoticed. That's when the hell started. Luke had never hit her, but the rage she'd seen in his pale blue eyes frightened her more than she'd ever felt. Even now it forced her to pull the blankets tighter around her. He'd forbid her to go to her weekend getaway. Called her a slut and a cheat. Said that if she loved him she'd want to be with him always. The words echoed as if they'd just been spoken.

Then he'd looked back over his shoulder in the direction Bash had gone and said. "How'd he know where you were going? He meeting you up there? You guys got something going on, you whore?"

She'd frozen. Never much of an actress, the pure fear of being found out had likely been written on her face.

He'd slapped her then—open-palmed across the cheek. "That bastard," he'd muttered. Then to her, "You'd better be here when I get back. We're not done yet."

"Yes, we are." All or nothing. She'd done it then and had, for a few short hours, felt as if she'd accomplished a miracle.

Luke had jumped into his work car, a beat-up Monte Carlo with a built-up engine, and roared off.

Outside her half-open window, she heard the low, guttural growl of a high horsepower engine with little holding it back. The wild stallion of cars. When it revved, blasting RPMs that nearly shook the ground, she jumped.

That was real. Not imagined. And it wasn't Bash's Chevy, either.

She jumped up and raced out of her room.

Bash already had the front door open and stood on her front steps, staring at the vehicle stopped on the street in front of her house.

She gasped, her body trembling with the same level of fear she'd just pulled out of her memory.

In the circle of light cast by her twin front porch lights and the glow of its own headlights, sat a blacked-out Corvette. The paint was dull, matte, and try as she might, she couldn't see even the shape of a person behind the wheel. That much tinting had to be illegal. Side pipes crackled as the car was revved, its front end rocking at the power of its engine.

"What—who—where did *that* come from?"

"Get in the house, Bree." Demanded, not asked.

That caused her to bristle. "My house. I don't need a guard dog. This a friend of yours?"

"No. Get in the house."

Naturally, she had to push against the hand he'd put out to stop her. As soon as he touched her, the rear tires of the 'vette caught pavement and sent up a white plume of smoke that enveloped the car. The engine raced.

She stood there, enraged and fascinated by this show of horsepower. But for God's sake, it was now nearly one in the morning! "Who is it? I've a mind to call the cops."

"Won't do any good," Bash retorted. "He's gone. And if I'm right, uncatchable."

Yeah. Right. Men have such big egos about their cars. "Nothing's uncatchable." But the smoke was starting to fade, and the car was gone.

* * * * *

Bree sat at her kitchen table the next morning and wondered if she'd dreamt the whole thing.

Bash was gone. The blanket she could have sworn she'd tugged out of the hallway closet for him was now back there, as if it'd never left. Nothing was out of place, not even a dirty cup to prove he'd gotten a drink of water before exiting the house.

She'd even tossed on her sandals and rushed out to the garage. No Bel Air sat in the main bay, just her lawnmower. Even the lantern was where she'd put it.

Nothing, except the twisted knots in her gut, could convince her that Sebastian Bernecchi had returned to Holtsville after a two-year absence and *happened* to have his car break down while driving through her subdivision.

Riiiiiight.

She sipped more coffee.

What was he doing here anyway?

Eyeing the phone, she tried to think who would know all the comings and goings in this little town. Kelly, probably not, but Randi—named so appropriately— probably would. Thing is, did she want to advertise her lunacy if she was wrong and it *was* a dream?

She dialed anyway.

"Randi? Bree. You busy for lunch?" Even as she asked she looked at the clock, then at her clothes and tried to figure how much time she needed.

"Uh-oh. Something's up. You always make *me* coerce *you* into going to lunch."

Hmm. Should she ask her now? Nah. She wanted to see her face and judge for herself if she was telling the truth, or knew. "Yeah. I need some scoop and you're the rumor queen of the county."

The snort wasn't ladylike, but then again...it was Randi she was talking to. "Now you've got me curious. Meet me at the mall at noon. I've got some shopping to do. Left wing, center court."

The mall wasn't even in this blink-and-you'll-miss-it suburb, it was nearly a half hour drive south. But maybe that was good. Bree agreed and raced to the bathroom to get ready — and made sure she was fully dressed this time.

Chapter Three

"So what's the deal?"

Bree chuckled as her perfectly coiffed friend raced up to her and grabbed her arm. Randi wasn't bad, at all. At least once one realized that there was no such thing as a secret around her and she wore the title of news spreader like a medal. She'd been right by Bree's side since Luke died. In that case, Bree realized, she didn't go spreading details of how well, or not well, she took Luke's death.

"I figured you'd know what was up. I, uh, saw a face from the past yesterday."

"Really? Who?"

Bree waited to say more until they'd gotten into line at the Italian fast-food restaurant.

"He—"

"Shit," Randi whispered. "I know what you're going to say. I saw him, myself, just a day or so ago. That guy looks just like Bash, doesn't he?"

Just like Bash? Her memory was foggy, but she was sure he'd mentioned his name—and he'd known the garage. He'd talked about Luke, about the car. No, it was definitely Bash. But since Randi didn't know about what had happened between her and Bash—no one did—and she didn't want to give her any clue or otherwise the slightest hint of gossip-worthy information. "Hair was different."

"We can't have cookie cutters, though, can we? So spill, where'd you see him?"

"He drove past the house." That was more than enough information. The butterflies in her stomach were already spoiling her appetite.

Seemed good enough for her friend, who placed her order, then leaned against the stainless steel counter and said, "Shame we lost Bash. I think he was quickly becoming Holtsville's hottest bachelor."

"And there were, what, maybe ten in the running for that title?" She slid into the bright red and white booth. "No biggie, Ran, yesterday was just a bad day. I think I overreacted."

Randi touched her hand. "Nonsense. I can't even imagine what you've gone through. Reminders like that probably twist the knife."

Like right now. See? Even her friends thought she had reason to feel guilty. "Yeah."

They dug into their food, all the while, Randi talking about people they'd gone to school with and the general goings-on. Bree barely listened to the news of how the preacher's son got arrested for drunk driving. She was busy trying to turn on the defoggers in her brain and visualize Bash's face. It was him, she knew it. Her senses knew it. But if Randi wanted to think it was a look-alike for whatever reason she had, then so be it.

"What's Kelly doing?" Bree asked, steering the conversation toward mutual friends. "She thinking of going back to school?"

"Beau's walking and almost potty-trained, so yeah, now that he can do day care, that's her plan."

"Cool. I need to go see him. He changes weekly."

"Ain't that the truth." Randi looked up over her straw. "You sure you're okay? You look tired."

"I am."

"Bree, doll, it's been two years. You gotta let go of it and live. Quit measuring everything by that part of your life. It's over. Move on. Hell, go find this new guy in town and get laid or something."

That jerked her chin up. Did she know? How could she know?

"Well, fine then, find someone. If you don't want this guy, I'll take him. Thought you'd done staked your claim, the way you dragged me out here to talk about it."

Bree made sure the air that left her lungs did so slow and easy, and didn't catch Randi's attention. She shook her head. "I've got no claim on anyone."

"You should date, you know."

"Yeah."

She knew, but the prospect just didn't appeal to her. It was true, there was only a handful of single guys their age left in town and most of them already had girlfriends or weren't worth a second look.

"Seriously." Randi pointed her straw at her, splashing brown drops on the white tabletop. "I'm calling Kelly as soon as I get in the car. We're going to have to drag you out with us."

"Sure." Agreeing now meant she could say no later. It wasn't that she didn't want to. She'd tried—and ended up sitting at a dark table in the bar while her friends laughed and danced. She'd never been one to enjoy that scene, but now it was nearly torture.

"Listen." She piled all her trash on the tray. "I'm gonna fly. Need to get a new outfit for tomorrow night and get home. Why don't you paint a smile on your face and walk around looking eligible."

Yep, sure. She knew exactly what Randi meant. *Eligible?*

Exiting the freeway ramp, Bree immediately started looking around for Bash's navy and white car—if only to prove to herself that she wasn't crazy. She hadn't dreamt it.

She even took the long way through town, stopping to pick up her dry cleaning and a movie for the long, boring evening ahead.

"What the..." As she turned down the street, she could plainly see a pair of black tire marks marring the pavement in front of her house. Her insides twisted as she remembered—the black car. Did this mean that it hadn't been a dream, either? Unless Bash had laid these down when he'd left—but how had she slept through that?

Blinding pain throbbed behind her eyes. She pulled in the driveway and cut the engine.

"Dammit." Her shoulders slumped when she saw her mother's pale blue sedan sitting in front of the garage. With her mother in it, engine running, likely for the sake of the air conditioning. She wasn't going to be happy. *How could she have forgotten?*

"Hi, Mom," she called and waved as she got out of the car.

"Brehann, weren't we supposed to have lunch today?"

Bree heaved a sigh and pinched the bridge of her nose. "Yes. We were. And I forgot. I'm so sorry. Did you still want to go? I need to run inside first."

"Are you feeling okay? You look white as a ghost."

"Headache." She hated to squint toward her mom. It felt so much better with her eyes closed. "Coming inside?"

Without waiting for a response, Bree fumbled with the lock and finally pushed out of the blinding sun and into the cool, darkness of her kitchen. After downing two painkillers, she turned to her mom. "I'm real sorry I'd forgotten. I had to meet someone and it ran late…" She sucked at lying. She'd completely forgotten. But no sense hurting Mom's feelings.

"Who did you meet with?" Translation—*Was it a guy*?

"Just Miranda."

"Oh." Her mother crossed her arms over her blouse. She was dressed as if she was going to church. Probably to pray for her daughter. No. That wasn't nice. Her mother loved her, even if she did often make her feel as if she were a teenager again.

"We've got that shower on Sunday, you know. Your cousin's expecting you to show up."

Cousin Barbara was having a baby. Bree'd managed to wiggle out of being in the wedding party and conveniently had plans for the wedding shower, but she knew they'd hogtie her and toss her in the trunk to get her to the baby shower.

Translation—*Mom wanted grandchildren.*

"Yeah, I remember. We were going to get a present, weren't we? Here." She dug in her pocket and pulled out a wrinkled ten and two ones. Lunch change. "You need more than that?"

Her mom waved her off. "I'll get it, you can pay me later."

"Sure?" Bree twisted to look out the window when she heard the loud exhaust. *Please, please don't stop here. Not now.*

The sound cut off and was followed by a squeak and then the slam of a car door.

Great.

Mom was going to love this.

Bree was tempted to burst through the back door and say *Ixnay on the isitvay*, but didn't. No need to make it look like she was hiding something.

Fact was, her mother had liked Luke—loved him. Thought that his intent to take Bree in and support her so she didn't have to work was wonderful. She pooh-poohed Bree's argument early on that she wanted to go to college, to have a career. Of course, her parents were old school. She couldn't fault them for that. It just wasn't for her.

Bash, on the other hand, had been termed *defiant* and *irresponsible* and *immature* many times by her parents. This usually happened after a visit to the garage, at which point Luke became the angelic, kiss-ass son-in-law-to-be and Bash, well, Bash was himself.

Bree thought it was funny. So did Bash. Luke often got upset, thinking that his buddy should kiss ass, too.

Now he was here, and Bree doubted it would be any different.

"You've got company," her mom said.

"Yeah. I know." She eyed the door, waiting for his form to block out the bright sunlight.

Mom lifted her eyebrow and stepped back to look out the door. "Something wrong with your car?"

Huh? "Mine? Uh," she stuttered, walking over to get a view of what Bash was doing out there. Finding him on the gravel, looking up under the engine compartment, she finished, "I think so. He's supposed to check it out. But I figured he'd take it in the garage."

"Then let me get out of here. It's not often one finds a mechanic willing to come to your house."

Which meant she hadn't recognized him. Yet. There was no way she was going to walk in front of her car and *not* see him. That ought to send her into orbit.

"Just a minute." Bree grabbed the garage key from the drawer and went outside. She took all four porch steps in one leap and skidding to a halt in front of Bash's half-hidden body.

"What are you doing here?" she hissed, nudging him with her toe. "Here, get into the garage. My mother's visiting." She let the key fall onto his chest. "Go, before she comes out."

"Okay."

She gritted her teeth as his noncommittal voice. "Did you know you've got a power steering leak? And several of these radiator hoses need changing. They're all starting to split."

"Great. Now go. Please?"

"Yeah, yeah." Bash stood up, towering over her five-and-a-half foot frame. She hadn't remembered him being so tall. No, take that back. Her eyes roamed the way the white T-shirt, now dusty and grease-smeared, tightened across the muscles of his chest and shoulders. Damn. He'd been tall, just not so wide. The years had been good to him. Her mouth nearly watered at the masculine physique before her.

"Brehann!"

She closed her eyes and hissed to Bash, "Go!"

Whimpering to herself, she turned back toward the porch, where she knew her mother stood with a disapproving frown. She'd get the speech about not trusting him and him taking advantage and God only knows what else. Bash's parents were from the proverbial "wrong side of the tracks" in her parents' eyes. Luke's mother had gone to church with her parents, that, obviously, was his saving grace, considering the two had lived next door growing up.

"Yeah, Mom?" She shielded her eyes and looked up.

"I-I-I…" She turned and went back in the house.

Bree followed, racing up the steps. Her mom's face was white. Probably the sudden heat along with the shock of seeing the face from the past. Surely her own features had mirrored that look last night.

"Are you okay, what's wrong? Here." She thrust a glass of iced tea in her mother's hand and pulled out a kitchen chair.

"Phew. Heat's bad out there," her mother said, her color slowly coming back. "A shock to the system after being in here where it's cool." Fanning her face, she blushed. "Hot flashes are normal at my age, but not like that."

Bree sighed. Good. Let her mother blame it on menopause.

"For a minute there…" She shook her head.

"What, Mom?"

"The young man working on your car. He looked like that hoodlum Luke used to hang around with."

"Sebastian."

"That's right. Can't say I found it a shame when I learned he was gone."

Bree poured another glass and downed it herself. She wouldn't do it, wouldn't take the bait, wouldn't argue as she had a few years ago. "Yeah, well, that's all in the past now. Perhaps you should go home and lie down."

Go, please. And so help me God, Bash had better be completely out of sight.

Bash stood just inside the garage door and listened to Bree's nervous voice as she walked her mother to the car and made sure she left.

"What are you doing here?" she demanded of him as soon as she crossed the threshold. "God, that was awful. She acted at first like she'd seen a ghost." She laughed, the sound practically echoing in the empty three-car garage.

"Sorry." The last thing he wanted was a run-in with her mother. That woman had something against him from the get-go. Probably something ignorant like her mom and his mom were high-school rivals or some shit. It had never bothered his friendship with Luke, and ultimately Bree. Nor did he expect it to now. "I came by earlier, you were gone, but there was a puddle where your car was parked." He shrugged and knocked a spider off a stack of shop rags. "How long has that been leaking?"

Her huge blue eyes flitted toward the door and then back at him. "I don't know."

"Have it serviced lately?" He walked around the garage, able to really assess what was here, and how…untouched most of it was. Why? Did she pine for

Luke, come out here and imagine him here? Or was she afraid, as she had been when he was alive? He had been so damn protective of his tools, there were days Bash couldn't even use them. Either way, from the lack of use of all this equipment, it was obvious she'd never tried working on her own car, though he didn't doubt she could.

"Down at Jay's place. That's where my dad told me to go. I had no clue, you know. Luke always did everything."

He doubted she was half as helpless as she believed. The kids at Jay's were young, but they wouldn't have glossed over a power steering problem like that. "So when'd you go there last?"

She winced. "About three thousand miles ago?"

Busted. He laughed. "Glad to know you're not perfect. You were giving me a complex."

She snorted. A cute, almost dainty sound, but he knew she meant it. And he was joking. She didn't cook well, for one thing. The more he looked at her, he couldn't remember all the other faults. What *had* Luke bitched about all those nights? God, there couldn't be so much.

"I'll get to it," he said. "I'll get the stuff tomorrow."

It never failed to steal his breath when her eyes lit up. The guilty smile pulled at her mouth until a tiny crease— almost a dimple appeared in her right cheek. "You don't have to. Really. I'll take it down there. I've got plenty of time."

"You don't trust me? I promise, I won't even charge you half of what those guys do. There's something I wanted to do this afternoon, so is it okay if I come early in the morning?"

Her face fell. His own heart reacted with a rapid increase in tempo. Dare he believe her body language, even when she didn't *say* she was happy to see him?

"Hey," he said, reaching out to lift her chin. "I'm not going anywhere this time, Bree. I've got some things I need to see to today, though."

"Of course. I'm sorry. You have your own life."

He couldn't understand her worry, but was relieved his explanation eased the creases on her forehead. "I will see you tomorrow, right?"

Bree nodded and met his gaze, promise shining in her eyes. "I'll be here."

Yes, she would. Just as she had been for two years, waiting for someone to pull her out of the past and into her future. Not that she'd admit that.

He stroked her cheek and tried to memorize her features. Hopefully it'd be enough to get him through the night.

The unmistakable sound of the Corvette soured his demeanor. Why couldn't he stay away? Why couldn't he leave him alone? Especially around Bree?

"Tomorrow," he promised, and got behind the wheel of his car. His eyes stayed on her as he turned the key, but his concentration was on the car drawing closer to Bree's house. "Now go inside."

He quickly turned around in the narrow area between the house and garage and waited at the end of the driveway.

Let him pull down the street. Let him try it. No way was that bastard getting to either of them. Even if it meant he had to sleep in his car in her driveway.

His eyes darted to his rearview mirror. Bree still stood there, at the edge of the garage, waiting for him to leave.

Why hadn't she listened? He could only wonder what she thought of the reappearance of the Corvette that had put on a show out front the night before. He took a deep breath and returned his attention to the street, waiting for the car to appear.

Bash patted his dash. His old Chevy was not a wimp. Besides that freaky incident with the coil wire, she was the best-running hot rod in town.

"C'mon," he said, gunning the engine. He clenched his teeth and tightened his fingers around the steering wheel. The nose of the 'vette was barely visible, just a shadowy hint of what was to come.

"You want me? Huh? You want her? Over my dead body, pal."

He gunned the engine.

"Bash!" Bree screamed when he nailed the gas. Gravel rooster-tailed up from the wide rear tires as he twisted out of the driveway at the exact moment that sinister black car roared past.

She ducked, shielding herself from the raining of rocks that tinged against the metal garage door and to avoid seeing what should have been an inevitable crash.

Dread curled in her stomach. She waited, every muscle tensed, her eyes squeezed shut.

Nothing.

When she finally lowered her arms, both cars were gone. No mangled wrecks with flames shooting through twisted metal. No smoke. No cars—period.

There hadn't even been any sound other than the initial squealing as Bash's tires cleared the gravel and grabbed on the pavement.

The only thing that even indicated they had been there were the twin black marks on the road and the lingering smell of racing fuel.

"Bash?" Rushing forward, she squinted up and down the street. How had they disappeared from sight so quickly? If they'd been racing, surely she'd have been able to hear them winding out gears long after they'd disappeared from view.

Nothing.

Maybe she was losing it. Maybe that black car hadn't been there. Bash had simply dropped the clutch too quickly on the loose gravel and kicked some up.

Shaking her head, she turned and closed up the garage.

* * * * *

The day and evening stretched into what felt like years. Bree busied herself with the household chores—even delving into the spring-cleaning she'd put off. But even as her hands stayed busy, her mind kept slipping into the past.

How ironic. Back then—everything was pre-Luke's death and post-Luke's death—Bree would clean house and dream of the future, when she could fill her days fulfilling her career.

"Damn." She closed the closet, the last piece of clothing put away, and dropped herself onto the bed. The ceiling fan rotated slowly, above her. It was almost hypnotizing to watch.

And even that triggered a memory flashback—to the first summer they'd been in the house, before they'd gotten the air conditioning fixed. One of them, Luke probably, had gotten the brilliant idea to install ceiling fans.

Yeah, it had been Luke. Just like it happened yesterday, she remembered the banter between the two friends.

"I'm not going up there, it was your wise-ass idea. 'Sides, you weigh less. I'd crash through the ceiling," Bash had said, laughing.

Luke probably weighed thirty pounds less than Sebastian, all in the chest and arms. Luke was wiry strong, where Bash had the football player build. Though even then she'd doubted the difference it would have made to the ceiling beams.

She'd mulled around, feeling helpless as Bash had stood on the ladder in the middle of her bedroom, holding up the fan and light unit. It had been blistering hot that day—twice as hot with no air circulating. She didn't want to know the temperature of the oven they referred to as the attic. All she'd been able to do was provide cool glasses of water and towel to wipe off their sweat-streaked faces.

Her breath caught as she'd remembered something that had happened that day—something she'd tucked away in the recesses of her mind. Rolling over on to her stomach, Bree giggled and kicked her feet up.

Bash had been making faces at her—rolling his eyes, then crossing them as if watching yet another drop of sweat slide down his nose. He'd lowered his voice and pretended to be a commentator at the "Perspiration

Olympics". She had pulled over her cedar chest to stand on, grabbed the rag out of Bash's back pocket and wiped his face. Their eyes had caught and for a moment she'd forgotten everything else.

Then another rivulet had snaked down his forehead and perfectly skied down the middle of his nose. He blew right as it fell off, causing it to hit her cheek. She had nearly fallen from laughing so hard.

"What's going on down there?"

Lord, she could still hear the echo of Luke's voice reverberating through the room.

Sitting up, she looked around, suddenly chilled. And just like when he'd spoken those words several years ago, her mood immediately sobered.

Bash's hadn't though. He'd been used to Luke and his sulking, suspicious moods. "Man, you've got to be dying up there. I'm melting. Brehann's upset that I'm dripping sweat on her new carpet."

Her eyes now flickered to the ceiling. That had at least seemed to satisfy Luke. Hindsight, being what it is, made her wonder what he had *thought* was going on in the room below him. Bash was on a ladder with both hands above his head, holding the fan. If he was worried…good God! Her face burned as realization hit her. Had Luke actually thought she was sucking Bash off?

She got off the bed and kicked the heavy wooden chest that sat at the foot of her bed. "Damn you, Luke, for ruining everything with your possessive jealousy. For finding a fucking way to even spoil my memories."

Of course, that summer she'd been blissfully oblivious to his controlling nature. She'd considered herself lucky to have a man who wanted to be with her and proud to proclaim her as his.

"...property," she finished out loud. Three years after she'd moved in, however, she knew she was just another item he owned. His to rule, control, use or ignore as he saw fit. Her opinion didn't count and man, oh man, did he get pissed when she wanted to do something without him. It was then she'd decided she couldn't do it, couldn't stay. She'd formulated a plan. First, she'd shifted her major in school and added extra classes and finished her Associate's degree in business management, heavy in human relations and accounting, rather than the teaching degree she coveted.

As if it had been a week before, not over two years ago, she recalled the first of hellacious nights she'd spent plotting her way out. The end had been in sight. School was almost done, her victory.

Luke had started drinking. Heavy. She hadn't ever seen him drunk until that year, and found him in that state more and more often—just more reason to get out. She was holding on until finals, just another week. Three more tests. Then she could go, leave everything behind.

She also suspected another woman. Luke hadn't even tried to touch her in over a month. That stung, but she didn't press the issue. It'd all be behind her soon.

Then she'd come home after one of her finals, excited that she'd done so well, and met with the brick wall that was her fiancé. He'd laid into her immediately, verbally only, but the insults and accusations hurt as much as if he'd used his fists.

Worse thing was, he'd berated her in front of Bash. She hadn't known he was in earshot, but was more than glad when he stepped in and led a stumbling Luke away, mouthing to her "Get out of here" as he did.

When she returned from her best friend's the next morning, Luke had been passed out on the living room floor. She left him a note, outlining her school schedule, and tried to concentrate on passing those tests.

Bash had been there, at her car, the minute she'd pulled in the driveway after the next three hour final exam. He was trying to warn her, she realized too late. Luke had charged out at her, kicking at the fenders and trying to lure her out of the car. Bash had turned around and done something she'd never imagined. He grabbed his friend by the shoulders and said, barely loud enough for her to hear, "If you touch her, I'll kill you."

Bree sat on the bed and rocked back and forth with her knees tucked up against her chest. A smile played at her lips, despite her finding nothing humorous about the memory. She owed Bash. He had given her strength. Faith. He had believed in her. He told her, and Luke, that she didn't deserve to be treated like that. It was Bash that saved her self-esteem and kept Luke from guilt-tripping her into staying.

Speaking of guilt. She got up and left her room. Standing at the doorway of the spare bedroom, she wondered just how long it'd be before the sharpness of the guilt went away. She hadn't wanted Luke to die. He had done everything he could for her. If she wanted something, he'd get it. People liked him. Her parents liked him. His co-workers had wonderful things to say about his kindness and generosity.

But she had tried to live with him. Lord, she'd tried. Those people who sang his praises never saw the Luke she had.

After a night of his apologizing and promises to trust, she went off to school for that last final, certain things would be fine. She needed only a few more days until she could leave for good. But that afternoon she came home to the very same situation. No way would she live like that.

She rested her head against the cool drywall, hating these memories.

That night she'd gotten the last word. Bash had proclaimed it the funniest damn thing she'd ever said.

Luke had once again accused her of cheating on him, of having a boyfriend and even boffing the teacher. She'd put her hands on her hips and unable to censor her words for the rage building up inside her, she'd retorted, "Well, it's a shame you feel that way, but since you seem to think I was out whoring around, at least I got an 'A' on that *fucking* test."

She'd stood tall on the bottom porch step while he'd turned stark-white and stomped to the garage.

Then she'd sat down and cried.

Tears fell now as she remembered all that she had wept for. The end. Years wasted. Scars on her heart. The fear of starting over. She had little hope, and nothing but a diploma to use as the foundation of a new life.

Bash had sat beside her. She had felt his presence, though he remained there without speaking for a long, long time.

Finally, she blurted, "I'm leaving him." A fresh assault of tears had wrenched from her throat, as if her very heart were being torn out. She couldn't understand how it could hurt so bad when she was certain she didn't love Luke anymore.

"I know," Bash had whispered. "I'll miss you. But you have to go."

She'd nodded and hiccupped. Then covered her mouth and laughed. He always made her feel better.

Bash's hand had slid over hers and squeezed. "You get to bed. Spare bedroom. Lock the door. I'll cool him off even if I have to hogtie him and turn the hose on him."

Despite Bash's attempts to subdue him, Luke had followed her into the house and proceeded to berate her in a way she didn't ever want to experience again. Bash had tucked her under his arm and threatened Luke again not to strike out at her. Instead, he'd struck out at Bash, then roared off in a wake of flying gravel. Bash had sworn to stay until he came back—to protect her no matter what.

That's when it happened.

Bree walked to the kitchen and leaned her tearstained face against the glass of the storm door. That's when she'd killed Luke. Maybe he hadn't died that night, but that's when she'd killed him.

* * * * *

She must have fallen asleep, though she didn't remember walking from the kitchen to the sofa. It ached, these potent memories, this confusion, this guilt. Ate her up inside.

The phone rang, jolting her out of her reverie.

"Hello?"

"Bree."

Bash's voice, but it was muffled and nearly unintelligible for all noise in the background.

"Bash, that you?" She plugged her other ear and blinked her eyes to wake herself fully. Damn the pounding of her heart that started the minute his voice was recognizable. She could barely hear him.

"I finished up what I needed to get done earlier than I expected. Can I come by take you for ice cream?" At least that's what she thought he'd said.

"Ice cream?" she repeated.

"Yeah."

"Um. Sure. Or maybe you could just pick up a couple of sundaes and we'll eat them here." She shouldn't be, but there was a little apprehensiveness about being seen in public with him. It was a small town. People talked, asked questions. She had no answers. Yet.

"I can do that."

She breathed a sigh of relief. Her skin fairly hummed with anticipation when he promised to see her within the hour.

Shit.

House was clean, but she was filthy.

Bree undressed as she ran down the hall, then turned around and retrieved her clothes. Lord, last thing she needed was a trail. She balled her thong and dropped it into the hamper.

Thank heavens she hadn't worn those panties last night. Talk about a peep show.

Now she faced a tougher question. What to wear now? If she chose something lacy, was she sending herself, and Bash…if he got to see them…a wrong message? Good God, why was she even thinking about that? He said *ice cream* not *make me scream*.

With a groan, she blindly reached into her underwear drawer, then grabbed clean T-shirt and jeans. It was Bash, not prom night.

She repeated that mantra while taking a shower. A cold shower.

Chapter Four

Bash circled the block twice before pulling into Bree's driveway. No sign of that 'vette anywhere.

Too bad there wasn't a way to put a bubble around the house. With a final look around, he climbed the steps and knocked on the door. Second-guessing himself? Hell, yeah, he was. What was he doing back at her house, so soon, if not asking for trouble?

She was waiting on the porch.

"Hey," she said with a shy smile.

"I'm not keeping you from anything, am I?" She smelled all clean, the airy fresh scent of her shampoo tantalizing his nostrils when she leaned to pull the door open.

"No, probably just another night with the remote as my best friend."

That worried him. "I thought you go out with your friends. You can't lock yourself —"

"You want something to drink? I don't have any beer, though, sorry."

He wanted to drink her up. The way she fluidly moved across the kitchen sent his thirst to a new level.

"Anything's fine," he said, letting his eyes linger on her curves. He didn't care if she did notice his attentions. He wasn't embarrassed by them. "The ice cream parlor was in the other direction. I came here first, to see what you wanted." And to convince her to go with him. "You sure you don't want to go?"

"Nah, that's okay. We can just stay here." She ducked her head and smiled, only allowing him to see her face for a moment before leaning into the fridge. "I've got cola. Regular or diet."

"Regular. You don't have to be so formal." He fumbled with his car keys to avoid staring at her ass. Those pants were hot. Really hot. This was why he wanted to go out. Anywhere. She was damn distracting.

"I'm not." Despite her words, her tone was defensive.

"I don't need a glass or ice. Or a napkin. Quit fussing over me." As she leaned over to pass the can of soda, her T-shirt gaped. Creamy skin that begged to be tasted tempted him from beneath the thin cotton. *On second thought, about that ice?*

"Sorry," she said.

He had to laugh, she was nervous as a virgin bride. Only she wasn't a virgin. Oh, why did he have to think of that comparison?

"So, do you want to watch TV?"

"Actually, I came to talk to you." He swallowed and forced his mind where it belonged. While he was in the car, the thought of explaining what he needed to tell her seemed easy. Now, staring into her eyes as they suddenly clouded in confusion, he knew it wouldn't happen tonight.

On the outside she appeared healed, but she wasn't. To test his theory, he walked directly toward her. She backed away, her eyes wide.

"Afraid of me?" he chuckled and reached for her hand. "Or having second thoughts about letting me back in your life?"

She chewed her lip. He wondered why he wasn't able to do that. They'd taste like strawberries, their luscious pinkness exploding against his lips with the flavor he'd hungered for, for two long years.

"Of course I'm not scared. Still trying to get used to the idea. It's so weird to have you here, but not—"

"Luke. I know. But he is gone, Bree. We have to accept that."

Her creamy throat undulated as she swallowed. She stared at the floor, as if searching for something. There were no easy answers.

"We need to talk about him."

"I can't," she insisted, balling her fists at her side. "You're right. He's gone. We should just talk about us."

Interesting. Bash figured she'd avoid that subject like it was leprosy. "Here? In the kitchen? I was hoping we could sit down, you know, get comfortable. You don't look comfortable at all."

That was the truth if he ever spoke it. Every muscle in her body looked to be rigid. He liked her much better the way she was the first few minutes of his visit.

"Come on."

Bree sat in the oversize chair. He chose the seat closest to her. Their discussion didn't need to be yelled across the room. "About us. What do you think about us?"

She fiddled with her hands, twisting them around one another. That same strawberry hue stained her cheeks. "Us?" she repeated. "You mean our friendship?"

She knew damn good and well what he meant. He countered. "You have sex with all your friends?"

Her reaction was textbook. Appalled. Insulted. He grinned and grabbed for her hands.

"How *dare* you?!"

"Does that mean I was the only one? That's a relief."

She tore her hands free and slugged him in the arm. That was new. She *never* would have hit him before. And she certainly never struck out at Luke.

"You're despicable."

"You're damn adorable when you mimic cartoon characters."

"I thought this was supposed to be a serious talk?" Bree sat back in the chair, out of his reach.

Serious? She wanted serious? Well, then. "You never did really answer me yesterday, when I asked. Do you regret what happened between us?"

He immediately wished he could take the words back, or rephrase the question. It sounded accusatory, not a question that meant something. And it did. One of the main reasons he had to come back, he had to know. Make sure the last two years he'd spent thinking about her hadn't been all for nothing.

"I-I—uh, I don't know."

Breath left his lungs. At least she didn't say "yes, definitely".

"If...if we hadn't..."

Fucked? Made love? Had sex? He didn't say anything out loud. He wanted her reaction. Leaning forward, he nodded for her to go on.

"If we hadn't gotten carried away, then, well, Luke might still be alive."

"And?" His muscles tensed in case she decided to smack him again.

She was right, though. But things wouldn't have been the same. Not for any of them. She was going to leave Luke, and he wasn't going to give up the idea of making her his. Never had a woman wormed her way under his skin the way Bree had. She had no idea of this, however, and he wasn't sure how she'd respond if he voiced that right now.

When she didn't answer, he prompted, "What do *you* think would have happened?"

The sky blue of her eyes was cloudy, her smile hidden. "I wish I knew. I wish I could go back and tell him—" She paused and looked up at the closed blinds of the window.

"Tell him?" Bash took a long drink of the cold soda, hoping to release the tightness in his chest. The possibilities of the answers to that question worried him. Maybe he was wrong. Maybe she wasn't as strong as he thought she was. What if she did regret their night together? What if she truly did want to spend the rest of her life with Luke?

"Tell him that I didn't do it in order to upset him and that it wasn't, you know, like we were having an affair or anything."

"Right." Ow, dammit. "But with Luke it might not have mattered. You know how he was. We did it. That's all he would have heard."

Her eyes widened.

"Bree, please, you know how irrational he got. Don't gloss over that."

"I thought he was your friend."

"Dammit, Luke would've told you the same thing. Admitting that doesn't hurt."

She frowned and got up. Once at the window, she whirled. "Is that your plan, coming here and dissing him to have a replay of that night?"

He certainly couldn't deny thinking about that possibility. But, no, he wasn't expecting Luke to be any part the equation. He got up and pushed his hair off his forehead. What was he doing here? Seems like he was saying all the wrong things.

"If I take you to bed, tonight or any other night, it'll be because you want to be with me as much as I want you."

He waited for a retort that went along the concept of hell freezing over. When it didn't come, he searched out her eyes. A vise squeezed his chest as he saw the glistening of tears there.

"Brehann?"

"Why *did* you come back?"

For her. But not for the reason she'd expect. "I needed to come home."

She swallowed and swiped at her tears. "Why did you come here? Why are you here now?"

"I missed you." He didn't hesitate at all before answering.

"So why'd you go? Why'd you leave me?"

All these questions and so many answers she wasn't ready to hear. "It doesn't matter now, does it?"

"It doesn't?"

"No. The past is the past. I came back because it's time to face it and move forward."

"Good for you." Her voice was shaky, but he guessed she was trying to sound sarcastic. "I didn't have the luxury of running away and hiding. I had to face Luke's death every day."

He spun her around, knowing his temper was showing on his face. He didn't care. She acted like he never hurt. She'd never understand the level of guilt he faced, the pain at losing his best friend, the tear in his heart when he left her behind. "You don't know what it was like. You couldn't."

He let her go and walked back to the couch and sat down, dropping his head into his hands. What the fuck? The whole night had gotten turned inside out.

"I'm—"

"*No, you're not sorry!*" He jumped up and dug his fingers into her limp shoulders. "I don't want you to be sorry. I want you to say what you feel and not regret it. I'm not Luke."

She stared at him, her mouth agape. He should have said he wasn't *like* Luke. But he hadn't, and now the woman in his arms looked up at him in disbelief. How to tell her that he liked her honesty and unedited opinion without comparing himself to Luke? The way it sounded, at least to him, was that he was stepping into Luke's shoes. Taking over. Assuming a place in her life she hadn't asked him to fill.

Bash waited for her to react, unwilling to do anything to chase her from his grasp.

She sniffled. "No, you're not at all like him." Her gaze left his, and he expected her to distance herself.

Whew. Maybe she hadn't realized his slip of words. He needed to slow down and not let high emotions take over his tongue. "I want you to remember one thing. I'm your friend. Okay?"

She bit her lip and nodded.

He breathed in relief. For once he'd actually said the right thing. Reaching around her, he gathered her up and pulled her close. Her cheek rested against his chest. He dropped a kiss in her sweet-smelling hair.

It was killing him not to tilt her face up and say, "Forget the friends stuff". He wanted more, so much more. But not when their conversations still revolved around Luke.

"Why does it have to be like this?" she asked.

Like what? "Life's rarely fair."

"It seems less fair now."

This woman was truly an enigma. "What does?"

"Us."

Sebastian's arms tightened around her. She seared the memory into her brain. This feeling of being wanted, possibly even needed — it nearly brought tears to her eyes.

Bash wasn't like Luke. She'd known that for as long as she'd known Bash. She didn't *want* him to be like Luke. Mainly because Luke wouldn't stand in the middle of the living room with his arms around her unless it was his version of foreplay.

A shiver shook her body.

Bash felt it. He pulled her back. "You okay?"

She nodded. But it was too late, the feeling was lost. Like a warm blanket being pulled away. She felt cold, exposed, vulnerable and afraid. Amazing how Bash could step in and erase all those things.

"Not mad at me?"

Mad? "Of course not." She wrapped her arms around her middle and looked around. Lost. Here she was in the middle of her own living room and she felt lost. "Let's go outside. I need some air."

He grabbed her hand as they walked out. His large, calloused fingers dwarfed hers. His thick hands were dark, both tan and stained from hours of working in grease and oil. Shiny slivers of scars marred the knuckles. Absently, she brushed her thumb over a long one that ran nearly the length of his forefinger.

"Why so quiet?" he asked.

"Thinking." As soon as she said it, she knew this conversation would fizzle into the stalemate, just like before. They could talk about the weather, about her job, about his. Ask about one another's families and avoid the subject that everything would eventually lead back to—Luke.

"About what flavor ice cream you want?"

He'd pull a smile from her one way or another, wouldn't he? "Not exactly."

"Bree?"

The shadows hid his features, especially his eyes. But his voice was enough to cause that tidal wave of emotion crash over her again. *Like that first night, when he asked her if she was sure she wanted to go through with it.*

"Mmm?" There was no need to close her eyes, but she did. Her senses were alive—the cool breeze against her cheek and lifting her hair, the tinkle of the wind chime at the corner of the porch, the scent of fresh-cut grass and late-blooming flowers. And the presence of the man in front of her.

Even though he didn't touch her, she felt him. She wanted him there. Never wanted to stand on this porch alone again.

"Okay, now what are you thinking?"

"Nothing."

"You sighed. You were thinking something."

Thank goodness there wasn't enough light for him to see her blush. And that he couldn't read minds. "I'm glad you're here, Bash."

Her heart thumped against her chest. There. She'd said it. He'd already indicated how he felt about her, so she wasn't even sure why she was so apprehensive or afraid he'd reject her feelings.

"Me, too."

He slipped an arm around her shoulders and held her against him as they stared out into the yard. Fireflies, the last of the season, sporadically lit up the bushes along the front of the porch.

"I don't think I've ever seen this place so quiet."

Funny, she'd gotten used to it. But just like that, just his words and she could visualize the blazing outside lights, the open garage doors, emitting unintelligible strains of the latest rock band. Occasionally pings of tools against concrete or the toolbox preceded the echoing curses of man against machine. "And I'd almost forgotten what it was like for it not to be like this." She reached up and swiped at the stupid tear that dared trickle down her face.

It's not like she really missed it. After all, back then she cringed, imagining their neighbor's reactions and wishing the guys had a little more consideration. She'd sworn she'd never miss it. Yet she did.

"I can't answer for you, but for me, all these good memories are tied up with the bad. Let's leave that stuff buried."

She nodded. Best advice she'd heard yet.

"I should go. It's getting late."

No! Not now, not yet. Bash made her feel...so alive. She entwined his hand with hers and prevented him from stepping away.

"I'm sorry, Bree. I didn't mean to start talking like that and upset you."

Did he not understand? Upset? She was going to be upset if he left, not if he stayed. "Don't go," she whispered. Scared, that's what she was, scared they'd never recapture a moment like this one.

"Bree, I can't—you know how I feel about you and it's just too—"

"Shh," she said, tugging him back toward the door and the dimly lit kitchen.

"Do you know what you are doing?"

All she knew was that she wasn't going to let tonight escape. She'd felt this way once—once!—before in her life and acted upon it. Did she regret it? That answer was crystal clear—no. Which told her that regardless of the consequences, she'd regret it only if she didn't act on her feelings tonight.

"Bree?"

"I was trying to decide if I'd regret it if I asked you to stay."

Maybe she'd felt brave enough to admit it because the darkness masked the blush that burned her cheeks. Bash's reaction was also hidden by the shadows.

"And?"

She took a deep breath, knowing that her answer could shatter any hope for their fledging friendship. "Come inside, Bash. Stay with me."

She turned and went inside, her heart thudding and her hands shaking. If he didn't follow, she'd be mortified. Oh, God, what had she done?

"Don't offer an invitation like that and then run away," Bash said, the screen door slamming behind him with a sense of finality.

Surely he could hear her ragged breathing and thundering heartbeat. When she turned away from the doorway where his voice had stopped her, words failed her.

His eyes were smoky and heavy-lidded. The planes of his face seemed more defined. His hands, Lord, those hands reached for her.

"Don't do this for the wrong reasons," he said, reaching up to push her hair behind her ear. "I'm not going to deny I want you. But…"

"Shh." She hushed him by placing a finger against his lips. He immediately opened his mouth and pulled it inside. Breath left her lungs. The edges of his teeth lightly held her finger in place while his tongue stroked up and down, teasing her with the vision of how his mouth might feel on another part of her body—a part trembling and throbbing from this tiny act.

"Can you give me all of you, Bree?"

She whimpered as he kissed her palm, then lowered her hand. Deep eyes met hers, imploring. There was nothing to do but nod.

She reached up on tiptoe, more than anxious to feel his mouth on hers. "Kiss me," she whispered, licking her lips. Hoping, trying to convince him to take her back to that place where there was no pain, no indecision. "Love me like you did before."

Bash stiffened. As she reached up to pull him closer, he stepped away. No! "Bash?" she gasped, searching his face. He wouldn't meet her eyes.

"We can't go back. Only forward. I'm not here to replay a stolen moment."

"Replay?" she gasped and shook her head until her the ends of her hair stung her cheeks. "I never want to go back to that. You have no idea how…" Even now, tears stung her eyelids and threatened to steal her composure.

"Oh, I think I do," he said. "There's no greater pain than wanting something you can't have. Then getting it, and having it yanked from your grasp."

She blinked and studied his face, her frown deepening. "I've never known you to be so…philosophical."

Bash's lips pulled up in a bit of a smile, though his eyes failed to reflect anything but a sad thoughtfulness. She wondered what caused him to look so…haunted. "When everything else is gone and you've exhausted yourself trying to understand why and how, you lay awake at night, so tired you can't sleep, and you think about it. Your life flashes before your eyes, and you learn how important things really are—"

"What *happened* to you?" It had to have been horrid, the way he described it. She felt cold and lonely just listening to him. The expression he wore seemed almost hollow, as if he were reliving it himself.

"Bash?" she prompted.

His eyes pulled back to hers and he blinked. Life returned to his eyes. "Sorry."

She leaned against his hand as he reached out and stroked her cheek. "No, I'm sorry," she said, feeling the ache in her chest. "I didn't know. I'm sorry for reminding you of that."

Taking a gamble that it was the right move—how could it be wrong when she couldn't imagine doing anything else?—she stepped forward and wrapped her arms around his middle and rested her cheek over his heart.

She was rewarded with the warmth of his arms encircling her shoulders. He dipped his head down. She sighed with contentment to feel his breath in her hair. *This* was what she wanted, needed for so long. It was almost as if somehow they had stopped being two people and had melted into one, held together by the glue they'd use to mend their broken hearts.

"Will you stay?" she whispered. The pressure in her chest made it impossible to take a deep breath. How did she live without this? All these months she'd remembered the heat, the passion, when this belonging seemed to be what she craved.

"As long as you need me." Bash stepped back and gathered up her hands.

With her heart near bursting no way was she going to let him spend one more minute talking about why or why not to do this—and just do it.

"Well, I need you."

He laughed. The vibration of the low, slow sound reached her and shattered any hesitation that still lingered.

As he led her toward the hallway, she couldn't stop mentally pinching herself. His hand was clammy in hers and squeezing a little tighter than she'd have liked.

Nerves. Not much different than the first time.

Oh, God. She was going to do this.

"Second thoughts?"

Bree wondered how he'd read her mind. "Oh, no. Just seems like a dream and I'm afraid of waking up."

He stopped and backed her up against the wall in her hallway. "You're awake."

She waited for him to say something else. But yes, he was right. She was so very alive. Her body hummed, her heartbeat echoed in the narrow hallway as she stared up into Bash's face.

Dammit, what were they waiting for? She smoothed her palm over his chest. Beneath her touch, muscles shuddered.

He wanted her. All the long nights of dreaming, hoping—wanting him—could be realized tonight. Her short-trimmed nails skimmed the muscles that bunched beneath the worn, white cotton. Her breath caught as his did. She felt his sharp intake of breath as his rib cage rose and fell under her exploration.

She didn't stop, afraid to wake up. What an incredible dream. The heat through the material, the sound of his heart thundering beneath…she could even smell him, a hint of musky sweat, the tartness of gasoline and the familiar scent of oil and grease. Closing her eyes, she reveled in the man before her.

"Bash," she prompted, tugging up on the material. Skin. She wanted to feel it burning under her touch.

His hands were trembling as he untucked his shirt and started to pull it upward. The hard muscles of his stomach were faintly defined under golden skin. But her eyes were drawn to the tattoo just above his left hip.

She touched it, then drew back, almost afraid the flames that engulfed the tiny heart would burn her as well. Try as she might, she couldn't clearly remember if it had been there before. "Is this new?"

He nodded and finished disposing of his shirt. "It seemed appropriate. For a lot of reasons."

His eyes clouded slightly, and she regretted breaking the magic of the moment.

She ran her hands over his stomach. The skin there was smooth. If she didn't look, she couldn't see that reminder that what had brought them to this point had been paid for in pain and tears. For that reason, she was determined to enjoy it, to make it a memory she could cling to for the rest of her life.

With her eyes and her fingers, she memorized the angle that his wide shoulders tapered into narrow hips. She didn't understand how those well-worn and low-slung jeans didn't just give in to gravity. He reached down and twisted the button loose.

Her mouth went dry. She licked her lips and stared at the trail of hair that disappeared into the vee of denim. Her nipples hardened, her sex flooded with moisture. It was as if that simple act alone flipped a switch in her body.

The featherlight touch she used earlier was replaced with fingers that kneaded muscle and grazed over flesh with her nails. She pulled him against her, then lamented not having removed her own clothing first, so she could feel the press of his hardened planes against her soft curves.

Finally, frustrated that he hadn't started exploring her body the way she did him, she placed her hands on either side of his head and pulled his face down to hers for a kiss.

Then she understood why.

It was like releasing the bull from the pen. A groan tore from his mouth as she pushed her tongue in through parted lips. He gathered her up so tightly it almost hurt, from a hand tangled in the hair at the back of her neck and the other hand pressed tight against the small of her back.

"Bash!" she gasped as he picked her up. Instinctively she wrapped her legs around his waist and clutched his shoulders. Fingers dug into her thighs as he held her up and pressed against his swollen cock. She could take him here, like this. Hell, she'd take him anywhere right now.

He, obviously, had other ideas. He took three steps to the left.

"Wait. No." Somehow she couldn't. Not her bedroom.

He stopped and stiffened, but didn't say anything. And didn't put her down like she feared. "Guest room?" he asked.

Dumbly she nodded and held on as he twisted around and backtracked toward the door at the other end of the hall. She nuzzled against his neck and tried to recapture a bit of the urgency that had seemed to escape when she had stopped him.

"Get the light," he said as he stepped through the doorway.

She complied, reaching out and bathing the almost sterile room in artificial brightness. It made her cringe.

"Okay, bad idea. My bed's not made and there are dirty clothes on the floor, but it's better than this."

"Good."

He didn't even pause to let her extinguish the light, but rather strode purposely back out toward her bedroom door.

The hall light was right outside her bedroom door. Bash would be able to see the bed without aid of the overhead light. Yet he still stopped. "Turn on the light."

"We can see." Not that she didn't want to see his glorious body in the full light. Memorizing every inch of his physique was one of her goals, but she'd sacrifice the brightness of four sixty-watt bulbs to trace the shadows with her fingers…and mouth.

When she didn't reach out for the switch, he growled and bumped it with his elbow.

Bree couldn't see what he saw. In her mind, she replayed the room, trying to remember just how bad she'd left it. How was it different than the last time Bash would have been in here? It wasn't unusual for him to step into the room. She could remember at least a half dozen times she'd let Bash into the house and led him to the bedroom so he could harass Luke until he got up out of the bed.

Those thoughts disappeared as he strode forward again. Straight past the bed and into the adjoining bathroom. He sat her on the counter and backed up, ultimately finding a seat on the edge of the tub.

"You're sure you want to do this?"

Was he kidding? He had to be kidding. *He* was having second thoughts? While the driving need had faded, she knew it'd take little more than a stroke of his calloused hands to prime her for his loving. She nodded and pushed herself off the counter. "I absolutely want to do this," she said. Mental images flashed into her head. Blood rushed directly to her groin and the sensations of extreme awareness revealed her arousal.

Bash stared at her, a funny grin on his face and his head tilted sideways. God, she loved that smile. It warmed her all the way through. She felt completely comfortable with him, confident even.

She slipped out of her jeans and kicked them toward the door. "You know what I think?" she dared to speak what just occurred to her. "We're too busy thinking and analyzing our own reactions and each other's reactions and we're not doing. I think," she paused and slid her hands down the side of her shirt, making sure to graze the sides of her breasts. They puckered as the fabric brushed over them.

She continued, holding Bash's smoky gaze and walking toward him. "I think we should just shut up and make love."

He got up, grabbed her and tossed her over his shoulder.

Chapter Five

Brehann couldn't fight. She was laughing too hard to put any power into her attempted punches. He raced out to the bed and tossed her down. The mattress protested and one of the pillows bounced off. She couldn't care less.

Bash's eyes never left hers as he hastily yanked down the zipper and stepped out of his pants and underwear.

Dayum! It had to be a dream. Men didn't look this good in person. Especially naked. She licked her lips—they had suddenly gone dry—and stared. Muscles were more defined on his shoulders than she'd remembered, and his chest and abs boasted more muscles and definition. Seeing him topless hadn't been that uncommon. But that was before—and in the garage. She wasn't looking at him as a lover.

It was below the waist that caught her attention. He was aroused and proud of it. His cock jutted upward toward her. She knew it'd be velvety soft, but from that distance it looked solid as rock. And huge! Would it fit? Was it that big before?

She forced her gaze downward. Nice thighs, lightly covered in a dark smattering of hair. The brightness of white against his light olive-toned skin pulled her eyes down much too quickly. She couldn't believe it.

"Leaving your socks on?" she laughed when he crawled up from the foot of the bed toward her.

"They're not in my way."

She squealed as he grabbed her ankle and slid her down the bed. "My, aren't you in a hurry." Just like her. God, if he didn't hurry up and touch her, she was going to explode.

"These," he said, reaching up and tearing her panties off. "Are definitely in my way."

"Bash," she gasped. She couldn't believe he had done that, yet was willing to sacrifice every pair she had to have him do it over and over. Shit, that turned her on.

"And this." He tugged at the hem of her T-shirt.

"Whoa. You're not ruining this." She wriggled out of it as quickly as she could and tossed it in the general direction of the hamper.

It didn't get far. His hands were already on her breasts—outside of her bra, dammit. That had to come off. Now.

"In the back," she urged.

"I'm getting there."

Not fast enough. "Don't rip that too. It's my favorite bra."

"I can see why." He leaned down and placed his mouth over the white lace, sucking her nipple through the fabric. Damn, that was good.

"Um…" There went her train of thought. Bash slipped his fingers beneath the bra and found the sensitive peak of her breast.

He paused. "Problem?"

"Take the damn bra off." Now.

"Roll over." He withdrew his hand. Why? What'd she do? Last thing she wanted was for him to stop. But she obeyed. Surely he couldn't stop now.

She waited to feel his fingers fumbling with the eyelet clasps. Nothing. "Bash?"

"I can't decide where to kiss first."

"I'm thinking you don't want to do this, that you're just teasing me."

He draped his body over hers, his cock jutting right against the crease of her buttocks. *Holy…*

On second thought…*that* was teasing her. She wanted that inside her, rubbing in and out of her wetness. She arched up against him.

"I want to taste you first. Every…"

Oh God. She trembled at the thought of his tongue rubbing over her clit.

"…last…"

A whimper escaped her. She arched up against him again, eager to feel the pressure of him against her aching pussy.

"…inch."

His breath was hot on her shoulder. Her body convulsed with tremors as he lowered his mouth to her shoulder and scraped teeth and tongue down her back diagonally, then back up, following the ridges of her spine.

"Is it okay if I sample here?" he asked, his tongue flicking fast against the nape of her neck.

No, lower. "Uh-huh," she murmured into the pillow.

"And here?" Tiny nibbles along each of her shoulder blades. Oh God.

"Yeah."

She wanted to scream stop, yet beg him to continue, all in the same breath.

"How about this?" The stubble of his chin was like fine grit sandpaper against the small of her back, his tongue traced velvety circles on the flesh. The contradiction of sensations left her breathless.

"Bash," she pleaded.

"You want me to stop?" He didn't bother to lift his mouth when he spoke, his lips grazing lightly as he breathed out just above the cleft of her ass.

No, no, no! "Don't stop." *Hurry.*

Bash backed up, licking his way over the swell of her buttocks and into the ridge of her upper thighs.

So close. Her nerves were so tight they vibrated with tension. Moisture drenched her as she anticipated his touch. Wriggling did little good. No amount of hinting or moaning could force him to plunge his tongue between her thighs and stroke her pussy lips and clit.

She was on fire. And he seemed oblivious to it. His leisurely ministrations to the sensitive flesh of the back of her legs and knees only made her more desperate. Sparks flew from point of contact. His fingers kneaded where his mouth couldn't. She'd die from bliss.

"Bash, please!" she gasped and writhed as he licked her ankle. It tickled, but in a way that made it vibrate through her entire body. Her nipples ached to be squeezed and suckled, her sex throbbed with the need to be filled. And he kissed her foot. Was he crazy?

"Get up here, now."

He chuckled. "On my way."

Christ. He meant to work his way back up the same way he'd gone down—just opposite leg.

Could she come without him touching her *there*? The pressure of the mattress below her barely grazed her clit, but it might be enough.

But then his hand snaked up between her knees.

Higher!

She panted and lifted her ass to give him ready access. God, she needed this. Didn't care about anything as long as he touched her. Now!

She clenched her teeth but couldn't keep from crying out as his finger slid inside her pussy. The muscles there immediately clamped onto his hand. She bucked against him, eager to feel him pump in and out of her.

"So hot," he muttered against her thigh.

"Please," she begged, gasping as his thumb rubbed against her clit. "I don't want to come without you inside me."

He growled, or moaned. She didn't know, didn't care, just that the primal sound of it sent a shiver of anticipation down her spine. He climbed up over her, his cock pressing against the inside of her thigh where she had wanted to feel his mouth.

Just another inch. She rocked up on her knees, granting him plenty of access to her wet pussy. She wanted to feel his every reaction as he finally breached her opening and sheathed himself fully inside her.

"Bash, I need it. I need you."

The head of his cock rubbed against her pussy. The room disappeared. She knew nothing but the sensation of his throbbing heat against hers. He guided himself inside. The sensation of his fingers opening her wide and the full, confident stroke as he buried himself to the hilt sent her to heaven. And she never wanted to come back.

Bash held on to her hips and tried to regain composure. He thought he might explode at the sweet feeling of her muscles clamping down on his cock. First he closed his eyes and reveled in the sensation of her creamy arousal soaking his balls. Then he opened them, craving to watch as he withdrew himself and plunged into her againand again.

Which he did.

It was more than he remembered and better than he'd ever dreamed. She gave herself to him—pushing back against him and whimpering as he speared her tight wet cavern. Her skin was flushed and glowed with sweat. He gripped her perfectly shaped ass, using his added strength to pull her back harder and faster onto his cock.

"Oh God, Bash. I-I'm…" her voice trailed off into a keeling cry as her body shuddered and spasmed against him. He let go of the reserve he held, increasing the tempo and thrusting until the world shattered around him and his seed emptied into her still quivering pussy.

Bash pulled Bree onto her side and spooned against her sweat-slicked body. Euphoria slipped away, gradually, despite his attempts to try to fight it. He didn't want to look around and remember he didn't belong in here.

She moved against him, the smooth skin of her buttocks cradling against his hips. He did so belong here, right here, with the woman he loved in his arms.

Why didn't fate see it that way?

"Bree, love?"

"Hmm," came her contented purr.

"Why don't you crawl under the covers before you fall asleep." Damn his practicality.

"I like this," she said.

He groaned. Why did she have to rub her backside against him like that? She was all dozy and he was thinking of anything but sleep.

For months he'd dreamed of this very thing, and here he was trying to figure out a way to leave without it seeming that he'd come for just this. *This* was a complete surprise, albeit a welcome one. But there was something out there in the night and he couldn't even remember if they locked the back door.

Truth was, he wasn't fooling anyone but himself. He would leave because it'd be too painful to stay, to imagine that he had a place here with her. He didn't. That was perfectly clear. And it had nothing to do with Bree's acceptance of the relationship between them. That could only make it worse. So yes, he was leaving. To protect her from even more pain.

He'd be back, again and again, until he found a way to tell her the reason he came back.

Once he did that, he'd never see her again.

Bree woke up when Bash lifted her higher on the bed and tugged the comforter from beneath her legs. She smiled, snuggling into the warmth he instilled into her body as he kissed her gently on the forehead.

"I'll be back in the morning, okay? You stay in bed and sleep. I'll be sure to lock up on my way out."

Too contented to argue, she lamented that he couldn't stay, but knew that would have been too good to be true. He'd be back. And they'd repeat what happened in here tonight.

Eventually they'd have to talk about where they were going and how they were going to handle it. In the meantime, she had one of the most amazing memories of her life to help her get to sleep.

* * * * *

"Huh?" Bree rubbed her eyes and squinted at the clock. First she'd thought she'd slept all night and Bash had already returned. But it was two in the morning. It couldn't be Bash. Unless it was an emergency.

She swung her legs over the side of the bed and stretched. She smiled into the darkness, feeling the stretch of muscles rarely used and the lingering satisfaction that can only follow a very good orgasm.

She flipped on the light and reached for her robe when she heard it again. A car revving.

As in, sitting in her driveway and revving.

Not Bash.

He'd have turned it off and rapped on the door, conscious of the neighbors and the time. Besides, he wouldn't scare her after that incident with the Corvette.

Goose bumps covered her skin and she couldn't pull the thick material of the robe around her fast enough. She turned off the light, sat on the bed, and stared at the window.

What did he want? Who was he?

One name came to mind, but she wouldn't put form to it. No. She didn't believe in ghosts. And if she did, weren't they just some...billowy, transparent vision that floated in and out of walls? Certainly they didn't drive souped-up classic cars and alert the entire neighborhood to their presence.

Of course it wasn't a ghost. Duh.

She grabbed the bedside phone and dialed 911. Her hand shook as she held it to her cheek and waited for the operator.

"There...there's a car outside, in my driveway, revving up his engine."

Calmly, the operator verified Bree's address and name. "Do you know who it is?"

"No! But I've seen the car in daylight. It seems to be...stalking me or something."

"Has anyone gotten out of the car? Did you get a plate number?"

License plate? She hadn't thought to look that one time she had seen it clearly. "No. The windows are dark and I can't see any..." she swallowed and blinked her eyes closed. "I can't see the driver at all, even a silhouette."

"Is it there now?"

Bree couldn't believe the woman couldn't hear it through the receiver. She didn't *want* to think it heard her and was becoming more aggressive. "Yes. In my driveway. Can't be more than ten feet from my bedroom window."

"I'm dispatching a car to your address, Ms. Williams. Do you want to remain on the phone with me until the officer arrives?"

Bree wasn't sure. If only Bash were here. Dammit. "Just for a minute. I'm going to walk over to the window and look out."

"Do you think that would be dangerous?"

And what was she going to do about it if it was? She hated this fear. It felt better that she'd made up her mind to look.

Outside, the engine raced. The windows rattled in their panes, creaking against aged wood. She jumped back and screamed as headlights came on and flooded her room with light.

"Ma'am, ma'am?"

Bree fumbled for the phone she'd nearly thrown in reaction. "I'm here. Oh God. Whoever it is knows I'm in here. As soon as I peeked through the blinds he hit high beams. The car's facing my window—he's sitting *sideways* in my driveway."

What was he going to do, run into the house? Why was he after her? What did he want? Just to scare her? Doing a damn fine job of achieving that goal, that's for sure.

"Stay away from the window. Can you get to another room? An interior room or hallway?"

Deep breaths. She had to concentrate on slow, easy breaths. *Why are you doing this to me?* she wanted to shout through the window. But she knew she wouldn't get an answer. Whoever was in that car was staying in that car.

Why?

"Ma'am, according to the officer, he's within a minute from your home. Is there a door you feel is safe for him to approach?"

Door. Right. "Probably the front door. The car is on the south side of the house, between the house and the garage."

"I'll pass that along. Can you see the front of the house, the road?"

Bree peered through the peephole at the front door. Nothing but black. Hell, some monster could be standing there with his finger over the hole for all she knew. "If I move the blinds. They're all pulled..."

"Wait—" Bree cut in. "I see headlights—a car. Coming down the road. It's him."

"The police officer?"

"Yeah." She could finally breathe. But it was short-lived. "Oh my God!" she gasped as the black Corvette, visible only in the reflection of her porch light—roared out of her driveway and directly toward the oncoming car.

"Ma'am? What is it?"

Bree tensed, waiting for the impact. But the sound of metal hitting metal never came. No sparks shooting off the point of impact, no screeching of tires.

"What's going on?"

Bree took a few deep breaths. What had she just witnessed? "The car left. Tore out of here without any lights on and, well, it looked like it was going to crash right into the front of the police car."

"It's gone?"

Bree's heart beat so hard and fast against her chest that she felt lightheaded. Pure exhaustion hit her body, dragging on her muscles and desire to deal with this any longer.

"Gone. But the police car is turning into the drive now. I'll go talk to him."

"Good."

Bree hung up and leaned the handset against her forehead. What was going on? Why was she being haunted...stalked?

She answered the rap on her door and flooded the kitchen with light. "Did you see it?" she demanded as soon as the police officer handed over his card. "From here, it looked like it was going to hit you head-on."

"See what?"

Ghost.

The hairs on the back of her neck stood up. She wrapped her arms around herself to ward off the chills. "The car. Black Corvette. Coupe, probably '66 or '67 model. If you didn't see it, surely you heard it. Exhaust is very loud."

"Ma'am, I don't know what you're talking about."

Shit. Had she hallucinated the whole thing? No. Bash had seen it the other night. He knew about it. In fact, he knew more than he admitted.

"Okay," she forced her lungs to fill, then empty. Fresh oxygen would calm her frenzied heart. "I was in bed, and was awakened by a loud car. When I got up, I realized it was very close. It kept revving up—I mean, loud. To the point the windows rattled and stuff."

God, she was rambling. And this sandy-haired cop stared at her without pen touching paper. "I called 911, and while on the phone, walked to the window to see if I could see a driver. The car blinded me with its bright lights. Then it must have noticed you were coming, because you weren't halfway down the road when it raced down the driveway. I could have sworn it nearly took off your front bumper."

"Ma'am, I—"

"It didn't have its lights on. It's black, all black. Not sure there's any chrome on it."

It didn't make sense. Yet as nice as this officer was, he didn't believe her.

"Okay, then. He's gone. You don't have to believe me. I'll get my camera out next time."

"It's not that I don't believe you, but surely you're wrong about the proximity it was to my squad car."

She shrugged. Maybe she had. It was dark, she was upset and she had been looking at it on a rather odd angle.

"Is there someone else in your house with you?"

Her stomach twisted. "No, why?" she choked out.

"I thought I saw something in the other room. You have a pet, a cat, perhaps?"

She shook her head. The room was dark, she noted as she turned around. Only the kitchen light was on, and it barely outlined the silhouettes of the furniture. Someone *could* be lurking there, behind the recliner. "Do you mind taking a look? I'm rather…freaked out about all this."

Thank goodness he seemed genuinely concerned about *this*.

They searched, turning on every available light and still using the high-powered flashlight to seek out corners of the closets and under the bed.

Nothing.

"My apologies, ma'am. I must have been mistaken."

That didn't make her feel any better. But she bid him goodnight and leaned against the locked door.

"That was fruitful," she muttered and rubbed her eyes. She was exhausted, but there was little chance she'd be sleeping tonight.

All the lights were still ablaze. Slowly, she circled the living room and turned them off, one by one.

Then she saw it.

Or rather, noticed something was missing.

She pulled the loveseat over and stood on the arm to see up onto the top of her bookshelf. There she'd kept several framed pictures, including one of herself and Luke. An old picture—one that was full of good memories. It always sat near the back to the left side, right behind the picture of her parents and grandparents.

Only right now, it faced backwards. She could see the gold of the outer edge of the frame and the darkened easel back that held it up.

What the hell?

So this was what those screaming girls in the horror movies felt like. She was hot, cold, it hurt to breathe. Her stomach wanted to turn itself inside out and her knees threatened to knock together.

All of that was multiplied by two when she realized there was no possible way to turn the frame back around without moving—likely removing and replacing—the other pictures.

Bash.

He had to have. But why? Could he be that...threatened by the one remaining picture of Luke in the house? And when had he had time?

Her gut twisted as she recalled why she and the cop had gone over the house with more detail than an appraisal company. Because the policeman had thought he'd seen something moving in the living room.

Bree adjusted the pictures, her hands trembling so badly the frames crashed into one another as she tried to set them back up. Then she counted, out loud, to ten as she pushed the loveseat back into place, extinguished the rest of the lights, and raced to her bedroom.

Chapter Six

Bash looked around the empty yard and frowned.

He'd mentioned he'd be back this morning. But he hadn't said when, or asked her plans. It was barely eight a.m. Truth be told, he was hoping to wake her, and see her smile, hair tousled, cheeks pink from sleep, as she opened the door. Lord knows he hadn't slept a wink, tossing and turning as he tried desperately to find a way to make this story have a happy ending. And had failed.

Now what?

Coming back here this morning had been necessary. He ached to see her, to make sure she had no regrets. The only regret he had was not staying last night. He could have. There was nothing to keep him from it. Well, almost nothing. Considering he hadn't even gotten close to admitting his secret.

The 'vette had been back. Those marks in the driveway hadn't been there last night. Why? What had happened? Did it have something to do with Bree being gone now?

She wasn't dumb. Eventually she'd quiz him about this car and he'd struggle to look her in the eye and admit the truth. And he wasn't sure he *could* tell her why it seemed to be targeting her. It should be after him.

Of course, once he said what he had to, both he and the 'vette would disappear. Then she needn't worry about it.

Just a slight dilemma there. He *wanted* to stay, both for sex and for the companionship.

Damn he'd missed her.

He looked toward the bedroom window, remembering how he'd left her, all relaxed in sleep. Those lips had been slightly parted, swollen from his kisses, yet he'd yearned to touch them again. He could almost live on the taste of her alone. But it wouldn't be enough.

A rumble behind him shot his blood pressure through the roof and caused his palms to sweat. This—this constantly looking over his shoulder stole any ability to relax. He had to stay on guard. All the time. He turned and waited to face his adversary.

But the car, truck actually—old blue Ford that had seen better days *and* maybe at one time even had a real exhaust system—cruised by without the driver even looking at him.

Pushing the unruly hair off his forehead, he closed his eyes. Wasn't hard, though, to visualize Bree out there on the roads and imagining that black 'vette coming up behind her, or crossing the yellow line and heading straight for her.

Why her?! Fury built up in him. Anger that he couldn't stop it, couldn't grab her and run away. No matter where they went, they'd be followed. That wasn't living. There were no answers.

He swallowed and paced the distance between the house and the garage. He should go. Bree was a grown woman and had survived, quite well, in the two years since he'd seen her. Damn shame she carried so much guilt, though. It was his self-appointed mission to rid her of it.

But what bothered him more than anything was that he could very well be setting her up to replace one kind of guilt and pain with another. Was it worth the chance?

* * * * *

"Brehann, you okay?"

She straightened in her chair and dropped her pen to the desk. "Huh? Oh, yeah. Sorry. Had, uh, I'm sorry..." God, she couldn't think. Of what she needed to anyway. Her concentration kept getting lost in daydreams and memories. "Someone in the neighborhood has a loud car— and was out late last night. Sounded like it was just outside my window." As a rule, she didn't get too friendly with people at work. Rumor control didn't make it past those double doors. Neither did the fashion police, she noted as Rosie Lykins rounded the side of the desk and sat down.

"Really? Too bad. You do look tired and drawn, and a bit too skinny. You need to eat."

Two months away from the attendance secretary hadn't been enough. Bree wasn't sure why this woman thought she was her best friend—or maybe best enemy was more like it. If Bree had a hair out of place, Rosie was almost excited to be able to tell her about it, and then expected to be thanked for it.

Where were Angela and Michelle when she needed them? Couldn't they find something for Rosie to do in these last few days before school got started?

Bree tapped the space bar and blinked at the information on the screen. She was dutifully printing book rental forms for all the kids enrolled. "Here," she said, biting back a smile. "You want to alphabetize these for me?"

As expected, Rosie sprang to her feet, the chair practically sighing in relief. No, that was mean to think that. Rosie was overweight, but the clothes she wore, like today's purple print top with navy skirt—and black shoes—emphasized her extra pounds and seemed to add twenty more. "Uh," she sputtered. "No. I've got plenty to do. Really."

"Where are you going for lunch?" God, she was a sucker for guilt.

Rosie took her eyes from the dreaded invoices and smiled at Bree. Lunch was at least two hours away. "Burger Magic has a meal deal that's hard to top."

Bree nodded, then sighed. "Let me know when you want to go." Rosie turned and headed back toward the front of the office. She'd intended to call it a day at noon. An afternoon nap sounded delicious. Being awake in case Bash wanted to stop by after work was even more appetizing.

Fifteen minutes before the lunch bell—everything was up and running in preparation for herding a bunch of hungry kids to the cafeteria even though it was still a few days before that would happen—Rosie popped her head around the wall.

"I guess that means lunch is off," she huffed, her face all in a perfected pout.

Bree groaned. It was a shame Rosie was like that. But it almost made her relieved, whatever the reason, that she didn't have to dread a half hour of listening to negative and sometimes bitter remarks. "Why's that?" she asked. Obviously it was her fault. If Rosie had gotten what *she* considered a better offer, she wouldn't have hesitated to let Bree know.

"You've got a visitor."

Bree stood. Her chair squeaked on the linoleum. "A visitor?" No one visited her. She straightened the invoices and looked up at Rosie to gauge who it might be. She hadn't recalled telling Miranda she was getting back to work this week. Bash was the only other person she'd talked to lately and, she bit her lip to keep from smiling, they hadn't done much talking the night before. It'd have to be an emergency to bring one of her parents or her brother here. Kelly? Again...only under emergency situation. She'd be more likely to call.

"Brehann?"

Her attention snapped back to Rosie.

"He's waiting up front. I wouldn't keep him too long, I think Michelle's eyeing him up for lunch herself."

He? Bree rounded the desk and followed Rosie to the main office.

"Hey!" she said once she caught a glimpse of those broad shoulders that tapered down into a narrower waist and hips. *Dayum!* Those jeans were snug, but not too confining. She didn't blame Michelle for looking. She was practically in need of a drool bib herself.

But then he turned and smiled at her, his face lighting up and his mouth and eyes creasing into the giant grin that melted her every time. "Give me your keys."

She'd give him anything as long as he continued to look at her like that. But keys? "Huh?" she answered. Had she missed something while recovering from the sight of his heavenly ass?

"Garage keys. Most importantly, your car keys."

Garage she understood. Her car? She tried to compose herself—she knew everyone in the office had stopped to witness this exchange. This time she graduated from monosyllabic response to repeating him. "My car keys?"

"I found you by following the trail of power steering fluid from your driveway, through the drive-thru at McDonald's and into the parking place here."

Oh God. That was bad. She dropped into the waiting room chair and stared out the window. She couldn't see her car, but Bash's Chevy was parked in the fire lane.

"And you need my keys to do what?"

"Fix it. How late are you working?"

She glanced at the clock, tempted to say, *this is it.*

He spoke before she could answer. "If you thought my car would be okay here, I was intending to nurse yours back to the house and see if it's just a hose that gave out. I knew that pump was bad, but I didn't expect it to die on you like this. Is it squealing? Hard to steer?"

"Uh...no." Sadly, this time it wasn't his devastating good looks that had her dumbfounded. She couldn't afford something major to be wrong with her car, but she couldn't afford *not* to fix it either. "Don't you have to work tonight?"

"Day off." He grinned. Her heart turned inside out.

A set of keys fell into her lap. A bottle opener for a key ring. Looked antique. As did the keys. Because they were. "Bash, I can't..."

"Don't tell me you can't drive a four-speed."

He didn't want to see her try. Besides, she'd pushed the clutch in — or tried to. It'd take all the strength she had. And then the fear of every other damn car out there between here and home. If something happened to it...

"I can, but I won't." She passed the keys back.

"You keep them, just in case. I'll be back here as soon as I'm done, then, okay?"

They were warm from his body heat. Silly, she thought, but feeling that bit of energy transfer from his body to hers, albeit through something as simple as a set of keys, made him feel even more part of her.

Shaking her head she stood up. Last thing she needed was to get caught up in emotions here. She had to think about her car. "I was toying with the idea of leaving now, well, in fifteen minutes anyway. Hold on." She ducked back to her desk to grab her purse, trying to will her nerves to settle. The looks he gave her...especially when he'd said he had the night off in that slightly deeper, raspy voice. Shit, she'd damn near creamed her pants. It didn't get past her that he wanted the car done now so they could be together later.

A few keystrokes and she was logged off the system. When she got back up there, Rosie had taken the seat beside Bash that she had vacated. A bit of a knife twist in the gut, yes, but she wasn't worried. She could just imagine Rosie wasn't concerned about making herself look good as she was about making Bree look bad. It was just her way.

"Ready?" she asked, plastering on a smile. "Rosie, I'm really sorry about lunch. I didn't realize my car was doing so badly."

"It's okay," she said, absently picking lint off her lap. "Another time."

Her drama wasn't lost on Bash. "I'm sorry, did I mess up your plans?"

Bree opened her mouth, but Rosie cut in with a purr, "Oh, you know, just us girls having lunch. You're much more important that I am."

Oh God. She really, really had tried to like Rosie, and honestly did feel sorry for her—everyone else avoided her like the plague, which of course, only made her worse.

Bash looked at her, obviously looking for her input. She just shrugged. There wasn't an easy way out of this without looking cruel. Or so it had seemed. "Where were you planning to go?"

"Burger Magic," Rosie offered.

Bash scowled. Bree nearly laughed at the look of distaste. He'd worked there as a teen, she recalled. Probably hadn't eaten there since.

"Why don't we try Rooster's?" Chicken place that had everything. And it was closer.

Rosie nodded. "I like Rooster's."

He nodded. "Then let's go. I'll drive, then drop you back here after and then we'll get your car home."

"Oh my Lord, would you look at this?" Rosie exclaimed, clutching her clasped hands to her chest. "My grandpaw used to have one of these. I remember how four of us could pile into the backseat."

Bash rolled his eyes at Bree and unlocked the passenger door.

Rosie looked at the door, then back at Bree.

She had something up her sleeve.

"Of course," she continued. "We were tiny things then. I don't think they designed those backseats for curvy women like myself. Now, Bree, you're a skinny one. Hop back there."

Bree couldn't believe it. Rosie wanted the front seat with Bash. She tensed, digging her nails into the palms of her hand while waiting to see if Bash reacted. When he didn't, she set her jaw and climbed in. Maybe she could loop the seat belt around her...dammit, this car didn't even have shoulder harnesses.

"I've never been in the backseat of one of these before," she commented, smoothing her hand over the leather. "It's awful roomy back here. Did you know that Bash?"

Let Rosie read between the lines. Bree had to work with the woman for the next ten months and had spared her the embarrassment of trying to fit in, and then back out of, the narrow crevice between the upturned front seat and the doorframe, but it didn't mean she had to get walked on.

Bash chuckled and looked over his headrest. "By God, you're right, Bree."

Rosie gasped and jerked the door closed. The resounding slam rocked the entire car.

"Easy on her now," Bash said. He stroked the steering wheel as if to console her and Bree could see the muscle in his jaw twitching. "She's a bit old and needs a loving touch."

Rosie muttered something that sounded like "sorry", but Bree couldn't tell for sure. She only wished she could see Rosie's face. From the sight of the side of her neck, she had to be blushing down to her toenails.

But who cared about that. Rosie would be Rosie and there was nothing she could do about it. Besides, Bash was here. He'd come for her. Her car, but that was a technicality.

The radio played softly. Some oldies station, far as she could tell. Bash must have been able to hear it, though, his thumb tapped against the steering wheel in time with the beat.

His hands. Her mouth practically watered watching them smooth around the wheel as he guided the car away from the curb. Sunlight reflected on the otherwise indiscernible hair on the back of his fingers. She ached to touch it, see it if was as fine and downy soft as it looked.

She clamped her knees together and sucked in a breath of air as she remembered how those fingers had stroked her body with the same reverence as he now gave his car.

"Warm back there?" he asked.

Understatement of the year. "Uh, yeah, I could use a bit of air."

Which almost made things worse. With the window cracked, the breeze ruffled Bash's hair. Damn she wanted to weave her fingers into it. It brushed against the collar of his T-shirt. Tempting her. Calling her. And there, beneath it, she could see the wisps of downy hair that curled against his neck.

Goddamn.

"What do you do at the school?"

Good thing Bash wasn't talking to her. She wouldn't have been able to string a sentence together.

Rosie scooted closer and answered, "Attendance."

Bree gasped. How dare she?

"Ya okay?" Bash twisted to look back at her.

"Sure. Fine. It's, um…a bit warm." She fanned her face in exaggeration.

His fingers encircled the wheel and squeezed, then he straightened and adjusted the vent. "Sorry. The air conditioning was taken out of the car when the engine was rebuilt. I'm a bit overheated myself."

Bree caught his eye in the rearview mirror. He winked. She damn near fainted. "Just open the window a bit more."

"Not too windy on you?"

She needed ice cubes to even think of cooling down. "No." Shit. Her voice cracked. "Uh, no. It's not. Feels good."

She didn't dare look up in the mirror at him again. From the view she had of the side of his face she could see the outline of the creases in his cheeks. That fatal crooked grin would do her in.

"So when does school officially start?"

Bree ignored the question, figuring Bash was simply being a good host and including Rosie in the conversation. She stared out the window. How far away was Rooster's, anyway? Why weren't they there yet?

She laughed to herself. Rosie'd probably snag the seat beside Bash at the restaurant too. Not that she cared. The pulse that throbbed through her body now, brought on by Bash's subtle flirting, was enough to chase away any doubts and jealous demons and wait out her turn.

Bash *might* have time to get her car fixed today.

"Your friend Rosie is…interesting." Bash watched Bree as she glanced over her shoulder.

"Eh, she's harmless enough, if you know not to take her comments to heart."

He had cringed when Rosie accused Bree of intentionally eating light to impress Bash. At least she hadn't seemed to let it bother her.

"Taste this," Bree said, shoving her straw near his mouth. "It's to die for. I've never had one of their milkshakes before."

Then again, it was rather ironic Bree had ordered the milkshake with her salad. Perhaps the comment had hit a nerve.

What a woman. He loved the way her expressions mirrored her thoughts—like now when her eyes widened as his mouth closed over the straw. He had been fighting the same carnal thoughts as she sucked the milkshake. Only he'd been wishing *he* was the straw.

"Ready?"

"Uh-huh."

Her eyes darkened and she licked her lip. Shit. That's not what he meant, but now *he* was more than ready.

"Leaving already? I've got an hour." Rosie walked back from the ladies' room and looked from her seat and back at them. "I was going to have dessert."

"Maybe another time," Bree cut in, polite but firm, "but Bash has been telling me he's got a lot of work to do on the car."

He nodded. *In* the car, actually. Bree's suggestion about that backseat had him thinking of just how to burn off those extra milkshake calories—and remedy the tightness of his jeans.

The ride back was solemn. He tried twice to make conversation with Rosie, but those abrupt one word answers reminded him of his mother when she was upset. No man's land there.

Bree, on the other hand, smiled at him whenever he turned back to see her. The wind tossed her hair back, the sunlight hitting it and making it look like a golden red fire. She was a dream come true.

Well, almost. There was just one small technicality standing between him and happily ever after.

* * * * *

"I'll be right behind you. But I really wish you'd let me drive it."

Bree shook her head and slid into the driver's seat of her car. "I'll be careful. Promise."

Stubborn. She didn't want to drive his car, that's what it came down to. "Pop the hood. I'll add fluid. It should be enough to get you home. But you've got to give me your word that you'll stop and pull over if that steering wheel gets too hard to handle."

Grimly, she nodded.

"Dammit, Bree. Let me drive this. You can get the Chevy home."

"I'm fine. Let's go before it bleeds all over this lot."

"Go. I'll catch up."

He turned to walk away, then thought better of it and leaned into her window and dropped a kiss on her surprised mouth. "Be safe."

Beautiful. Her cheeks glowed pink and she bit her bottom lip. "I will."

She drove conservatively. Too slowly in his opinion. As promised, he stayed on her rear bumper, even running a red light after she'd coasted through the yellow.

Good one, Brehann. I don't need a traffic ticket here.

But no bright flashing lights appeared behind him. They turned down the road leading to her house and he was just about to breathe a sigh of relief when her brake lights flickered.

What?

He tried to see if she was trying to signal him, but couldn't see past her headrest.

She slowed again, forcing him to downshift and coast.

Then he saw.

The car. The black Corvette.

In her driveway.

Waiting.

Bash's heart rate tripled. He straightened and gripped the wheel, eyes darting from Bree to the car and back.

She was barely rolling now. Good. Last thing he wanted was for her to put herself in harm's way.

He tugged the Chevy out of gear and rolled up beside her.

Pointing ahead, he yelled through the open windows. "Wait here. I'll see what the hell this is all about." He'd love to take a baseball bat to that car, but it wouldn't make a goddamn difference. "Be ready for anything. I don't know what this freak wants."

She'd listen. Her knuckles were white and she clutched the steering wheel like it was a life raft. Every muscle in her body was probably as rigid as the frame of her car. This car scared her. She'd seen it last night, Bash was sure about it.

What the fuck did he want with her?

The 'vette's big block engine revved, its exhaust hitting the gravel and sending up clouds of dust behind it.

He answered the same way, letting the thunder of the motor answer for him. He may have a heavier car, a smaller engine, but he had something that damn car didn't. Purpose. Motivation. He had Bree.

And no way was this bastard getting her.

Adrenaline soared through his veins. He breathed deep, stretching his shoulders. It came down to this, a face-off. Just like those western gunslingers used to do at high noon. There was just as much at stake for him as there had been for those old cowboys.

He was ready.

One last check of the gauges and he slid the transmission into first, holding the clutch down and bringing the RPMs up to midrange.

The paint of black Corvette glistened under the sun as it rolled out of Bree's driveway and faced off opposite him. Bash gritted his teeth until his jaw ached. This could be it. This could be the end. The last he would ever see Brehann.

No. "Come here, you asshole."

As if it heard his beckoning, the 'vette lit up its wide rear tires until the smoke erased everything but the low-slung silhouette of that car.

He dumped the clutch and stomped on the accelerator, bracing as the car launched forward in its own squealing tires and smoke.

"You can't have her," he muttered through clenched teeth. "You can't have Bree." He shifted into second without lifting his right foot. One mission. One possible outcome.

Or so he thought.

Chapter Seven

Bree screamed and tore at her seat belt.

Oh God. Oh God. The car, that evil, evil car had swerved around Bash at the last minute and was headed straight for her. Her fingers wouldn't work. Her eyes unable to shift away from the sight of that long, slanted front end aimed like a sword at her.

Damn the auto locks. Damn this car. She had to get out.

She slammed it into park and clawed for the door handle. Shit!

"Run!" She thought she heard Bash's voice, but the thundering, inside her head and the from the full-force charge of the behemoth V8 kept her from knowing for sure. But run she would.

She tripped and fell. Sharp needles of pain shot up both arms as her palms smacked the asphalt of the road.

"Bree!"

This time she heard it along with the squealing of tires. *Oh, Bash, please. Please stop him!*

She was going to die.

It was Luke. He was coming back for her. To kill her like she'd killed him. His ghost.

"Bash!" she screamed, picking herself up and racing across the road, nearly falling forward with the exertion. There she collapsed into the yard and rolled over, half crawling backwards, not wanting to see the violent crash, but unable to tear her eyes from it.

Bash was coming, he'd turned around and his car burning up the tires as it pursued the Corvette, but there was no time. No way he could stop it now.

But then she saw his intention.

Bash had seen her bail out. He wasn't aiming for the back of the 'vette, he was coming for her, a shield between her and this maniac that had it in for her.

Why?

"No!" she screamed and dropped her head into her hands, tensing against the explosion she knew would come. Kamikaze style, the maniac driving the 'vette would total her car. And his car. Why? Why? Why?

But there was no crash. No squealing of tires as the 'vette changed directions in some psychotic game of chicken. In fact—she lifted her head, finding only Bash's car idling on the curb in front of her. The 'vette was gone.

Gone.

She shivered.

"Are you okay? Bree…"

Strong arms pulled her up and into a cocoon of safety. "Oh God, I thought he had you. Thank God you got out of that car." He smoothed her hair back and studied her face. "Are you hurt? I saw you fall."

She shook her head. She didn't want to think about it. Didn't want anything but this—the comfort of his embrace—right now.

But he pulled her hands around and lifted her palms to him, cringing when he saw the blood seeping from scratches and the tiny bits of gravel that were still embedded there. He pressed kisses to her fingers.

"We've got to clean this up. Come on. You can walk right? You okay?"

She nodded. She didn't need his support walking to his car or his help getting into the seat, but she welcomed it. Facing death took the wind out of her sails. They'd get to the questions, and answers later. Right now she wanted to be safe inside her house, doors locked. Then maybe her heart would slow to a semi-normal pace and she'd be able to stop shaking.

Bash got in and released the emergency brake. "Come over here."

She slid over and let him drape his arm around her shoulders. "I'm here. As long as I'm here, you're safe, you got that?"

She nodded and closed her eyes. The kiss he pressed to her forehead was full of promise. "I'll take you home and come back for your car."

Huh? Her car? She leaned forward and looked past Bash.

Her car. Right where she left like. Just *like* she left it. Untouched. Door hanging open, interior light on, hell, even the seat belt hung down from the way she'd wrenched it off her.

"Bash," she asked, her voice barely above a shaky whisper. "What happened to the Corvette? How did it not hit my car?"

"Shh."

A little stronger now, she pushed away from him and sat upright. "Wait a minute. Tell me what's going on here. What *is* that car?"

"It's not real."

Oh, no. She wasn't going to deal with *that* story. "It is real." In fact, she'd see the car do damn near the same thing to that police car last night. She wasn't hallucinating or imagining. She'd seen it. "That car is as real as this one."

Bash put the car in gear and backed down the road and into her driveway. "It is and it isn't."

She'd been right. It didn't make her feel any better, in fact, she was hoping he had some explanation that eliminated those spooky thoughts from her mind. Was he saying it was a ghost? "It vanished, didn't it?"

"Yep."

Shit.

Maybe there was something scarier than facing down death. Realizing she was facing a ghost.

He killed the engine and opened the door. "Get in the house."

She shook her head. "I can't."

His hand shook as he pushed the hair off his forehead. "Okay," he said, obviously realizing why rather than asking her. "Keys in the car?"

In fact, if she was right, her car was still running. She bit her lip and nodded. He was going to walk up there. Leaving her alone in this car. Without even the ability to hide under her bed.

"Don't move."

As if.

Bree pressed her fingers to her temples and held her eyes tightly closed. Nightmare. Had to be. Some crazy, messed up creation of her imagination.

"Please, please, please," she chanted. But when she opened her eyes, she didn't see the ceiling fan rotating slowly or the light slipping in through the gaps around the blinds. Nope. It was real.

Lunch seemed like it had been hours ago. It'd been days since she'd been to work. Well, of course she was freaked out. The only thing that might have freaked her out more was to learn that it wasn't a ghost, but an alien driving that car.

"Oh, God, don't go there." She forced a laugh, a nervous, hollow sound in the empty interior.

"Bash, where are you?" She knelt on the front seat and stared at the opening to her driveway through the back window of the Chevy. What if the 'vette came back while he was out there? What if it ran him over while he was walking to her car? She hadn't heard anything, but honest, had she been listening?

Oh God. *Oh, God.* No. No way was she going to deal with burying another…special person. Her heart couldn't take it. They'd have to bury her too.

She didn't realize she'd been even holding her breath until she let it out when the nose of her car turned up into the driveway. Bash pulled it up in front of the garage, then came back to get into the Chevy.

"Here," he said, handing over her purse.

She didn't like the pale color of his face or the tightness of his features. "What? Where are we going?"

He fired the engine and tore backwards out of the driveway.

"Bash, no. Let me out. I can't do this." Remembering how Bash had barreled down the road, straight into the path of that car had nearly killed her. Being *in* the car surely would finish the job.

"Relax. We've got to get some power steering fluid and I want to order a new pump. Yours is shot. Would you rather I have left you here alone?"

"No." No hesitating there. No sirree.

"C'mere."

Ignoring the fact that she should have worn her seat belt, she sidled over until her hip was pressed against his. He had to reach between her knees to shift. She didn't care.

"You know what happened back there, don't you?" She swallowed and stared out the window, afraid to see the truth on his face.

"Not really. But I'm starting to get an idea."

"But you think you know who—what that car is, don't you?" Deep breath. She knew. Even if he wouldn't admit it. She knew. In her heart she just knew it was Luke coming after her. But to hear it out loud? The hair on the back of her neck stood up.

How the fuck to answer that? She'd never accept the truth. No one would. Hell, he wouldn't have, if someone suggested such a thing. "There's so much I need to tell you. Right now is not the time." He turned at the red light. They'd be at the parts store in less than two minutes. He wasn't starting this without finishing it.

"Tell me about what?"

Damn it. He wanted to punch the dash. This was wrong. All wrong. He hated the timid fear that weakened her voice and probably tore at her heart. His own broke over and over, every time her smile faded.

"About me. About these last two years."

Her face fell.

He focused on driving and parked the car near the back of the lot, taking up two spaces. Before getting out, he turned to her, practically pulling her up on his lap. "I'm not going to mince any words here. I love you, Bree. I've loved you for years. Only now," he hesitated, trying to find the words to make her understand the depths these feelings went to. He sucked at this. "Now I need you. It's the only way I can say it. You are the only thing that keeps my heart beating. I'd never hide that or lie about it."

A tear slipped from her eye. He reached up and smoothed it away. "Tell me that was a happy tear."

She sniffled and nodded. "I know. I do know you love me. You don't need words. I feel it. But I'm scared. I couldn't bear to lose you. And…" She sniffled and looked out the window. "That still seems so possible."

He squeezed her hands, silently vowing to do everything possible not to hurt her, not to ever give her doubt. Yet it was in vain. He had more love to give her than she'd ever imagined. The one thing he didn't have was time.

"Stop crying, sweetie. The people inside will think I'm a mean 'ol boyfriend."

Her eyes searched his, perhaps startled by the word, the commitment of it. He wasn't afraid of commitment, not at all. Luke had been such a fool. Such a damn fool.

"Sorry," she said and wiped her eyes. "I'm a mess."

"You're a damn strong woman. Beautiful, brave. You're not a mess. I am. Being around you makes me all a mess inside."

Her face glowed as she smiled at him. She needed to hear that, just as he needed her to know, without a doubt, that it wasn't lack of love that would come between them.

"So?"

"You're such a bully. Let's go."

She got out on his side, immediately grabbing his hand and not letting go. If only he didn't have the Corvette, and what it meant, eating him up inside, he'd be the happiest man on the planet.

Walking into this auto parts store was revisiting the past. The shop had the same smell — that of used machinery and new rubber, of oil and the slight tang of grease solvent. He and Luke had practically lived in this place — not a week went by when they weren't here, even if was just to see what new goodies they'd gotten in.

This time things felt a lot different. Bash wondered how he'd be received, and even more, how Bree would react.

"Well, isn't that a sight for sore eyes," said Hank as they approached the counter. Bree's hand tightened around his. Probably meant she hadn't been in here since Luke died either.

"Hi," she said shyly. "I need a...what?"

Bash saw her straighten her posture as she turned to him. "Power steering pump."

"Power steering pump," she repeated to the manager at the counter.

"You gonna change this yourself?"

"I've got help." Bree looked back at Bash. He nodded and smiled.

"Your new boyfriend know what he's doing?" Hank lifted an eyebrow and looked Bash up and down.

Bree gasped, then turned to him. He could see it in her eyes. *He knows you. Say something.*

"I've worked on cars a time or two."

"Boy, there was no one like Luke, though. He was magic with those vehicles. Never saw a car he couldn't fix."

If Bree didn't release his fingers she *would* have to do the work herself, because he'd have no feeling left. "We'll do okay," she said, teeth gritted. "Do you have the part?"

"Coming right up."

Bash leaned in close and whispered in her ear. "Stay right here. I'm going to go get fluid and some other supplies."

Her creamy throat undulated as she swallowed and her nod was barely perceptible. Freeing himself from her grip felt like saying goodbye, despite the fact he was simply walking across the store.

She noticed. People didn't recognize him. She'd ask. He walked away to get away from the strange stare he received. Hopefully Bree hadn't noticed the guy just down the aisle of parts who turned pale when he saw him. Maybe taking her out wasn't such a good idea. Leaving her at home, however, had seemed even worse an option.

"Here," he said, placing several items next to the cash register. "I got this." He stopped Bree from opening her purse. "Don't even worry about it."

"But…"

Don't say my name. "We'll break even later. Okay?"

He wanted to kiss those pouty lips. But not here. Not when these guys were acting as they were Bree's self-appointed bodyguards. Apparently he wasn't the only one she'd charmed through the years.

"Brehann?"

"It's okay, Hank. Can't say I've had anyone willing to pay my bills before. I might keep him around a while."

They all laughed at that and the tension seemed to fade. At least until they got outside.

Her voice was low. "Why didn't they recognize you?"

"I guess they'd forgotten what I looked like. Besides, Luke was the one who always went after parts."

He popped the trunk on the Chevy and placed the box and bag in the spacious cavity. When he looked up, he found her staring at him, her eyes shooting sparks.

"They remembered me. I haven't been in there since, well, since before…"

"But you've been in town. They likely knew that. They weren't expecting me, especially with you. I think they were too busy trying to figure out how to act than to worry about me."

She didn't buy it. Not only had these men—men who had waited on all of them countless times—not known it was Sebastian, her mother and Randi had even failed to recognize him. Said it *looked* like him.

What the hell was going on? "There's something funny about it."

She got into the car on her side and sat on her own seat. No way was she wrong. So what was it? Why didn't people know? Did she just know him that well that the changes of two years were invisible to her? Was he at all right, that they hadn't expected him to ever show up in this little town again?

"You swear you're not lying to me?" she asked.

"That hurts."

"Dammit, Bash, you walk into my life on the exact anniversary of Luke's death, stir up emotions I thought I'd buried with him and now I'm dealing with Kamikaze stalkers in souped-up hot rods and the fact that no one in this town knows you except me."

She watched him, hoping to find some reaction, some answer in his features if he wouldn't voice them. His chest rose and fell, his fingers tightened on the wheel. But when he looked at her, his eyes were clear. "I'm not lying, Bree. It's me, Bash. You've got to know that by now."

There was no doubt. This was her Sebastian. He affected her exactly the same as he had years ago. If for that reason only, she had to believe. "But there's no coincidence that the 'vette appeared when you came back."

His forehead creased. His lips tightened. She was right, dammit. Why did she have to be right about that?

"He—it's followed me for the last two years of my life. I don't think it will stop until it gets what it wants."

"What's that?"

"Me. And now you—probably to get to me."

"Bash." She didn't feel so good. Her stomach twisted and all the blood seemed to drain out of her body. Breathing became a chore.

"Dammit, Bree." His words were far away and she was barely aware of the sensation of being pulled across the seat and into his arms. "I knew this was too much for you to understand. You're so strong, so capable. Don't give up on me now."

It was a nice darkness that beckoned her, one that promised peace, quiet, and no black Corvettes out to do her in. But there was no Bash there. And she wanted him.

"I'm here. Sorry." The last forty-eight hours had taken their toll. Bash, the 'vette—several sightings, none of them good—lack of sleep and now this? "I don't think I'm as strong as you think I am. I can't do this."

Just make it all go away. For two years she wondered about turning back the clock. Back to that night Luke died. Could she have prevented it? Or maybe just postponed it.

"What are you thinking, sweetie?" he smoothed her hair and pulled her head onto his chest. There his heart beat in a steady, soothing rhythm.

"That this is so messed up. Why? Why does fate have to be so cruel to us? Why can't we just forget the past and I can have you, you can have me and all will be fine?"

His face said what she knew too well. It just wasn't possible. "The past molded us. Right now we have each other, and personally, I'm tired of spending time worrying about the future. Let's get home and lock ourselves in your garage. I promise you one thing. I will not let that 'vette get close to you. As long as I'm around he can't get you."

She wanted to believe. God, how she wanted to believe. But what about when he left? "Stay with me then. Move in with me."

"I can't."

He answered that too quickly. She couldn't read his eyes, as he was focused on the road before them. She'd ask again, though. At least then she could feel some level of security.

Damn, she hated this. Two years of living alone and now she was afraid for night to come and to be all alone.

She half-expected the menacing black car to be in her driveway again, but all was quiet when they pulled up.

"Go in the house and get the garage key. Lock it back up behind you."

She nodded. He was being careful, that was all. Nothing to worry about.

Right.

They worked like islanders preparing for a hurricane. She quickly cleared out the second stall so Bash could pull the Chevy in, and then her car. The big door squealed and labored as it closed, sealing them off from the outside world.

"C'mere," he said, standing at the trunk of his car. Without hesitation she walked over to him. Instead of handing her the bag from the supply store, he pulled her into his arms.

"It shouldn't be like this. Dammit, Bree, you deserve better than this, but it's all I can give you right now."

She feared he was going to tell her something she didn't want to hear, some revelation that he wasn't staying or that it was all a lie.

Instead he lowered his mouth to hers and left her body trembling with the raw emotion conveyed by that brief touch. If that was all he could give, it was more than enough. So much more.

"Every minute with you feels like a miracle. I can't believe it."

"Believe it," she whispered, staring at his mouth, willing for him to kiss her again. Kiss her until her toes curled and everything else melted away. She wanted him to take her to a world where nothing else existed. "Kiss me, dammit. I don't want to wait all day."

And he did.

She closed her eyes and welcomed the heat of his body against hers, the way his tongue thrust between her lips and stroked her tongue, waking up nerves long dormant. Her body tingled, like she had a high fever.

Yes. This is what she wanted. What she needed.

Reaching up she laced her fingers in Bash's hair and held his mouth to hers as she kissed him back, invading his mouth and meeting him—their tongues tangling and warring. She wanted to blank it out, erase everything. Everything. She slid her hands down his chest, barely feeling the muscles there, grasping, rushing.

"Stop."

She backed up, chest heaving. "What?"

"This isn't you. What are you doing?"

"Loving you."

"No, you're not. Whatever that was, it had nothing to do with me." Bash pushed his hair back off his forehead and walked to the other edge of his car. "Don't use me."

A chill filled the contours of her body where Bash had been pressed against her, but it compared little to the emptiness in her heart. He was right, dammit, picked up on it immediately. She was using him. "I'm sorry. It's not what I intended."

"What are you trying to do?"

She leaned back against the back door of her car. "I don't know."

"You do. You were a woman on a mission. It was rather sexy, but your heart wasn't in it."

Sexy, huh? She looked up at him through her lashes. His snug jeans boasted a bit of a bulge. Now *that* was sexy. So he hadn't been unaffected. "It should have been you and me from the beginning. Luke should have never been in the picture."

"You can't—"

"Oh, I know we can't change it. But it's the truth. I thought I loved him well enough, but somehow that ended. I can't tell you when or where, but at the end, I didn't love him at all."

"I know. And you did the right thing by trying to get away. That's what I mean, Bree. You're strong, you can do what you set your mind to do. You always have. I'm so proud of you for being able to rebuild your life and be self-supportive. You can't know how worried I was that I'd either find you here, living in the past or worse, yet, gotten pulled into some rebound relationship because you couldn't be alone."

No, she'd stayed here. Why? Bash had populated her thoughts and she'd left the light on in the room of her heart for him. But did that keep her here, in this house? No. She'd hadn't the courage to leave, she needed the familiar, the comfortable. But she'd made it hers, erased as much of Luke as she could. "Rebound relationship? Hell, it took me months just to go to the mall with the girls. I still haven't been on a date. Unless, of course, lunch today was our first date."

"With Rosie along? I don't think so. But dates are for getting to know one another, and we got to skip that part."

"Did we? Do I really know you, Bash?" She looked up at this man that had been in her life since she was a teenager and realized she really knew very little. Where did he stay now? Where had he gone for two years? What had brought him back, really? It couldn't be her. Not her alone.

"Better than anyone else. You know the important stuff. You think I'd let my pals or co-workers hear me talk all mushy like this?"

"Oh God," she laughed. She could just picture him, greasy from head to toe, manhandling a forty-eight inch pipe wrench, saying, "My heart just melted man, one look from her and I turned into goo".

"See? So maybe you don't know I prefer strawberry over chocolate or vanilla ice cream, that I can't stand the smell of roses or baby powder and I'm really left-handed, but was forced to do everything right-handed because my dad was convinced society frowns on southpaws. Or at least, they did when he was in school."

"You're kidding me."

"Not either." He held out his hands to her. "Have you seen my handwriting? That'll be proof enough."

She hadn't. Had no clue how he signed his name. Learning these tidbits made her feel closer to him. "What else. I want to know everything."

He laughed. "Everything? I'm not talking about myself any longer."

"So show me."

That crooked smile appeared. The creases on the left side of his smile deepened more than the right, exposing just a few of his perfect teeth. That smile was more deadly than a firing squad. She loved him. Plain and simple. She had fallen in love with him all over again.

She stared straight into his eyes, dark stormy eyes that hid his emotions with a cloudy blackness. They didn't scare her, didn't warn her off. She walked right up to him. "Show me," she whispered. "Show me what I don't know about you. Show me how magical both your hands are."

"All of you. I need all of you."

"Anything you want."

Their eyes remained locked as he reached out and cupped her breast through her shirt. Her body trembled, her nipples immediately tightening against her bra, aching to be loose.

Those skilled hands rubbed both peaks, teasing them, plucking at them until she gasped the pleasure that spiraled down the center of her and set her on fire. Her natural moisture dampened her panties. Just the feel of the cotton against her swollen and sensitized pussy lips was already igniting a need inside her that Bash's fingers could turn to flames with one touch.

"So beautiful."

He pulled at her shirt, slipping it up over her raised arms. She shivered a bit as cool air hit her heated skin.

"More beautiful than I remembered." The back of his fingers traced over the skin exposed at the top of her bra, dipping into the crevice and then back up, nearly to her collarbone. She moaned at the exquisite torture.

She kneaded his biceps as he pressed a kiss to her shoulder, then spread a line of fire all the way to the edge of that white lace...but no further. Dammit. She squirmed and tried to push him to the sensitive peaks that needed his attention once more.

Was he laughing? She pulled back and looked at his face. He was! "What's so funny?"

"You."

She groaned. "What?"

He went back to feasting on her flesh, kissing all the sensitive spots and making her crazy with need.

"You just wait," she warned, catching her breath as his chin lightly grazed her nipple. "I'm gonna torture you so bad."

"What?"

Shit. His hot breath might have even been more erotic than his mouth. It went right through the thin material. Her breasts ached, they were so tight and neglected.

"What?" he said again, half-laughing.

"Stop that." Yet she couldn't help but laugh—one that ended in a whimper as his thumb strummed one peak. "You're killing me here."

"Oh, can't have that now. I'm not nearly done."

With that he pushed the material of her bra aside and pressed a kiss to the tip. She arched back, reveling in the sparks that shot through her whole being. Her breasts had always been sensitive yes, but never, ever had she thought it was possible to come just from having them suckled. "Bash!" she gasped when his teeth slid over the peak and pulled. It went straight to her core. Muscles there clinched and spasmed. So empty. She whimpered and tried to draw his hips nearer, to feel his erection rocking against her.

"You're getting way ahead of me here."

"Can't help it." Please stop. No, don't stop. Please…

"I'll catch up."

Sure. Uh-huh. But she knew he would. She'd make sure of it.

His hand smoothed over her breasts again, calloused palms just the right texture to shoot her to the moon. "I need to get rid of this. Turn around."

She shivered as his hands stroked her shoulder blades and then traced her spine up and down. *Hurry up, dammit.* What was taking him so long? Did he like to punish her like this?

Finally she felt the clasp loosen and the weight of her breasts released from the fabric. Instead of turning her around, he pulled her back against him. *Damn.* His cock was rock-hard against her ass. Pity there were several layers of clothes in the way.

Whatever comment she thought she was going to make about clothes was lost when his hands slid up her rib cage, tickling her, but then rested on the underside of her breasts.

"Have I told you you're beautiful yet?"

"Mmmm." *Quit talking and touch me.*

"You are. Your skin is so soft, so perfect. I'm afraid to break you."

"You are trying to kill me." That's it. Enough. She grabbed his hands and lifted them to her breasts, squeezing his fingers around them and leaning back into his erection.

"Easy." He pushed her hips forward. "I've got an idea."

Great. He'd just teased her, stripped her topless and was probably going to suggest they get to the power steering pump before finishing this. A whimper escaped her throat. She was going to explode first.

"It's a good idea."

She turned around. "Does it involve you taking your pants off?" If she could get him that far, she could get it done.

"Maybe."

She crossed her arms over her chest and tilted her head. "Maybe?" What the hell was maybe? His pants were threatening to blow the zipper out and he was talking maybe?

"Bash…"

"It certainly involves you taking your pants off."

Hmm. Now that thought had some merit. At least it was in the right direction. "I need to know more."

"Dear God, I've never negotiated sex before."

"It won't be the last time."

"Lord help me, woman."

Chapter Eight

Bash grabbed her and pushed her back against the rear quarter of the Chevy and assaulted her mouth with unsurpassed greed. Bree raised her hips, rubbing against the front of his jeans, eager to have his huge cock against her bare pussy, then pushing inside.

She moaned. Her legs threatened to buckle. Between his skilled tongue, his roaming hands and her carnal thoughts, she wasn't going to need *anyone's* pants to come off.

"Dammit, woman. I *had* an idea."

"What? I didn't do anything."

He didn't answer. His fingers fumbled with the waistband of her pants. Finally she pushed them away and did it herself. "There. And you wanted *me* to slow down?"

"Shut up."

His fingers skimmed just inside the waist and then tugged down. She wriggled her hips to help him.

"Jesus, woman. Who's killing who here?"

She looked down. Oh. That's right. She'd put on her lacy lavender thong for today. Nothing wrong with hoping. Still. "My panties?"

His hand reached for them.

"Don't you dare rip them."

His lips curled upward. Damn, was he sexy. She couldn't take her eyes off his face as he stroked the silky center and then almost reverently ran his fingertips over the lace that outlined it. He looked so intense, so caught up in the moment, she swore it felt almost like worship.

Then he bent his knees and kissed between her breasts. His hot tongue felt like velvety fire as it slowly dipped lower and lower, circling her navel and plunging in. She cried out and gripped his hair. Damn, what was he doing?

Her pants were at her knees. She couldn't step out of them or spread her legs. Caught. Captured.

Tortured.

His mouth was at the waistband of her skimpy panties now, dipping just under the material. Thank God he'd pushed her against the car. She'd never be able to stand while watching his dark head descend lower and lower.

"Bash!" she screamed, unable to bite back the shock of his hot breath permeating the material at the juncture of her thighs. Oh God. Her knees were jelly. She closed her eyes, unable to focus anyway, just clutching his thick, dark hair to the part of her that ached with need.

His tongue stroked over the material. Thick, heavy, wet strokes. She whimpered and pushed against him. It was so good and yet left her so unfulfilled. She needed more than just the pressure and heat of his mouth. She wanted it on her, in her.

"Oh God," she gasped and leaned her head back against the cool metal of the car as his mouth dipped even lower, his tongue pushing inward, toward that spot. It grazed her clit, pushing the soft cotton against her. Did he have no clue the level of torture he took her to?

"You're so sweet."

"You're so mean." How she got those words out, she didn't know. There was no thought, no rationale left. She'd cry, beg, anything to have him continue—no, remove her panties, hell, let him tear 'em off—*anything*! "Take them off. I need—"

"Need what?"

She half-sobbed as he lifted his face to look up at her. "Don't stop."

"Stop what?"

Oh, please...please.

"I just want to hear you say it. I want you to ask me to finish it."

He wanted to hear it? She'd write it in blood—*after* he was done. She looped her thumbs through the strings at the waist and pushed down, shoving the thin scrap of material to join her pants at her knees. "This," she said, fisting his luscious thick hair and shoving his face into her pussy. "Lick me, Bash."

His moan vibrated through his lips onto her skin and caused her body to shudder. *Damn.* The lights blurred, mixing into a kaleidoscope of color. All that she knew was Bash's hot breath ruffling her intimate curls. She tried to spread her legs, but it was in vain.

The first touch of his tongue sent her into orbit. He slipped it between her lips and stroked, barely able to touch that nub that seemed to hold every ounce of her need.

The moisture on her thighs wasn't from Bash. She was practically dripping for him. Her pussy ached, throbbed, yet he simply grazed the core of her with his mouth.

"Don't move," he said.

As if. The car held her up, her body suspended in some state of utter arousal. She watched him as if it were a dream.

Bash opened the door of his Chevy and pushed the front seat forward. "Get in," he said, tugging her arm.

Walk? She looked down.

He laughed. Dear God, his face was damp from his erotic kisses, she was swollen and drunk with need and he laughed! But then he let the front seat drop back into place, picked her up and sat her there.

She closed her eyes as he pulled off her shoes, then pants. She sat there, in the front seat of his car, completely nude, completely defenseless. And he looked at her like she was queen of the world.

"Get in the backseat," he growled, reaching for the button on his jeans.

He didn't have to tell her twice.

Once there, alone, she started thinking about what they'd started. She felt her face go hot. Good God, had she said that? Sneaking a peek out the side window, however, bound and gagged any hesitation to finish this off.

Bash pushed his way in between the seats and reached up to pull the door closed. "Now," he said, that devilish crooked smile melting her into putty. "Where were we?" His eyes darted immediately to the Y of her thighs.

One of them moaned. Probably her. It was just about the only reaction she could have mustered to the way he twisted her in the seat and settled his head between her widespread legs.

Fuck, she was good. Bash slid both his hands under her ass and lifted her pussy up to his mouth. She squirmed and bucked beneath his tongue, but it only made him more determined to take everything she'd give him. Her cream poured over his tongue as he lapped.

He loved the way she fisted her hand in his hair and held him there, thrusting upward as he fucked her with his tongue, then pulled away as he caught her clit between his lips and suckled.

This was a side he hadn't seen before. While she was responsive in bed, she hadn't been this...hot. He wasn't complaining. Gently, he nipped at the inside of her thigh then the other, smiling against the wet flesh as he waited for her to demand her orgasm.

Eyes glazed over, hair mussed and cheeks flushed, she was the most beautiful creature he'd ever seen in his life. Her eyes followed him as he lowered his mouth back to her, spreading the lips of her pussy open and plunging two fingers inside. As she rose up against his hand, he flicked at her clit. His balls drew up as her slick walls closed over his hand and pulsed in response. She gasped out something he couldn't understand.

But he didn't stop. He was going to make her come—make her flood his mouth with her juices and then he was going to do the same to her. "I'm gonna take it all, baby. All."

He ratcheted his fingers in and out, twisted them slightly as he alternated between sucking her clit and massaging it.

Damn. He wanted to crawl up and plunge his cock into her and pound her into the trunk by way of the backseat. Based on her reactions, she probably wouldn't mind.

"Bash, I-I..."

He vibrated his tongue and continued to stroke in and out. He could feel it, the way her walls gripped at his fingers and poured cream all over his hand.

Close…so close. Just a bit more…

Ah hell.

He pushed her back a little farther and climbed up between her legs. She panted and whimpered, even tried to push him back down to finish the job. He couldn't. Not here, not when she drove him nuts with the way she reacted.

Fucking backseat. Too damn small. There was no way to stretch out his legs. But he'd make it work.

"Bash, please." Bree slipped a hand down between her legs and massaged the swollen nub above her slit.

The leather stuck to their skin. Christ, he needed to be sheathed in that body. Watching her touch herself just made his need that much worse. "Fold your knees up," he growled, his patience slipping.

Thankfully she complied while trying to pull him down on her. He leaned in, his body shuddering as his cock pressed against the wet flesh he couldn't wait to invade.

"Bree, I can't…"

Fingers dug into his hips as she lifted herself up and swallowed his cock.

Breath tore from his body. So deep, so wet. He belonged here, inside her, feeling her clamp down and pull ecstasy from him, drop by drop.

Her body ground against him. Gripping her thighs, he held her still and thrust into her, again and again. Stopping wasn't an option. Her gasps became cries, her fingers tearing at his skin as the passion took over and they were simply passengers on this spiraling trip to the edge.

Her scream echoed around him. He cried out just seconds later as she pulsed around him, her come spilling out as he thrust one final time, exploding so hard within her that she had to feel the hot flood inside.

Feeling returned to his other extremities. Muscles ached, and the cramp in his hip might be terminal. But the hum inside his body was his primary focus—that and the beautiful, sensual woman beside him who unfolded her legs and curled up against his chest.

It nearly brought tears to his eyes. This was heaven.

* * * * *

"Where am I?"

Bash stroked her hair away from her face as she blinked up at him with her not-quite-focused eyes. He grinned down at her, so in love with the gentle innocence on her face. "Backa my car."

"Oh," she said, blinking again, then rubbing her eyelids. She pushed off his lap and looked around. "Oh!"

"Oh?"

"How long was I asleep? God, I'm sorry."

The blush just added to her beauty. He wanted to say she didn't need to apologize, but he'd hate not to see that flush on her face again. "Just a few minutes. You needed it. But you snored. *And* drooled on me."

"I did not!"

The play of merriness in her eyes contradicted her shocked denial. He played along. Had to. It was the way they did things. "Did so. See that?" He pointed to a drop of moisture on his thigh. "Right there's proof. As for snoring, Christ, I'm surprised the windows didn't rattle loose."

"Dork!" She laughed and slugged him.

Nothing like the thought of a naked wrestling match. Unfortunately they were still trapped in this miniscule backseat. "Hey now!" he yelped, capturing her flailing fists and pulling her up onto his lap. "That any way to treat the man who just gave you the best sex of your life?"

Bree tensed. For a moment, his heart stopped. Shit. Had he said too much? But then her lips tightened and eyes narrowed. The telling factor was the way the corner of her mouth twitched.

"Best sex of my life, huh? Not a bit egotistical, are ya?"

She was going to get round two of earth-shattering orgasms if she didn't quite quit that wiggling. "You said it. I rather like knowing that."

"I really think you're making it up about me drooling. And I don't remember what I said about you, but it wasn't meant to swell your head." She tapped between his eyes.

"Am not."

Playful as their banter was, he knew damn well she felt his growing erection and was shifting intentionally to position her ass right over it. How was a man supposed to think, much less win this round of verbal sparing, under such conditions?

"If I'm right," he groaned and held her hips still. "You said, 'Never. There's nothing before…ever'."

He intentionally said it in a monotone. *She* had practically screamed it and moaned while her pussy had all but swallowed his cock.

Amazing how she smiled so angelically as she rocked over him. Her juices flowed over him, leaving him heady with the musky scent of sex and aroused female.

"So, from that," she continued, oblivious to his pain. "You derived I said you were the best I've ever had."

That's exactly what she meant and they both knew it. Now it was some sort of challenge to top it, to get her to admit it once and for all. He prayed he had the stamina.

"Oh look." Bree bent over, reaching for some unseen and likely invisible item of interest on the console. What it did was allow for her to sit on his lap with his cock nestled right between her ass cheeks. As she reached forward even farther, he could see the glistening pink lips of her still swollen pussy.

Damn.

He was instantly as hard as if he'd gone months without release.

"You're asking for it."

Without waiting for her answer, he grabbed her hips and lifted her up, held his cock at the dripping slit and then let gravity bring her back down—onto him.

"You bet I am." Bracing herself with the backs of the seats, she lifted and then lowered—the friction as he slid between those tight walls hot and torturously slow.

Lifting his hips did little. He had no leverage. And while he could pull her down a little faster than she lowered herself, she slid over his cock with the same mind-blowing slow pace. What had he done? Handed her the power, the reins to this horse, and man, oh, man was she breaking him down.

He licked his lips as he watched those pink lips stretch around his thickness, leaving it glistening with their intermingled juices. What he wouldn't give to shove his tongue there and lap them up, tasting both of them. He'd kiss her, share it. Would she like it? Would she lick it up as greedily as he would?

The answer was obvious and it caused his balls to tighten up against him with the fullness of his next load of come. He looked up, away from where their bodies became one. It'd drive him crazy if she were on top in bed. He could imagine her smoky gaze on him, her golden hair with its sexy red highlights curling around her face and spilling over her chest—but it wasn't long enough to reach her breasts. For that he was glad, he wanted to see them, rosy nipples jutting out at him, begging for his touch.

Unable to resist, he reached around and cupped them, treasuring the low moan that accompanied her pressing their weight into his palms. He kneaded them, closing his eyes to focus on increasing her pleasure. His pleasure was at her mercy. She whimpered one plea and he'd be over the edge and filling her up with his seed.

She ground against him, her tempo finally increasing. The side-to-side motion with him fully impaled inside her was hot as hell. Arching her back, she pushed against his lap, taking all of him in.

That fiery hair tumbled down her back. She was a flame and quickly lit him until the heat threatened to engulf him. Her body convulsed, her moves like molten lava, sensual, smooth and out of control.

He rolled her nipples, pinching until she cried out, then reached between their joined bodies and spread her pussy lips. When her exposed clit rubbed against his balls, she cried out and shuddered against him, her inner walls a velvety vise that practically sucked the come out of him.

"Bree," he said, wrapping his fist around the base of his cock and holding it up and letting her use it to find her release. She rocked back and forth, then up and down. While he watched. It was a wonder he held the finale at bay as long as he did.

"Come," he commanded through gritted teeth as his cock throbbed in his hand. Cream flowed all over his lap. Her pussy literally dripped with it. "I'm going to shoot this inside you, all hot and wet. Feel me come."

He grabbed her hips and pulled her down onto him, holding her still as he released the dam and flooded her trembling cunt with all he had.

She moaned and touched herself.

Shit. His cock twitched, waking up almost instantly. That was hot. Damn hot. "That's it. I like it when you make yourself come that way."

He pulled her back until she reclined against his chest. Looking over his shoulder, he watched her nimble fingers rub her clit. Her hips shifted, rubbing against his still hard cock. But this was like watching her masturbate. He could probably come all over again just being allowed to see this.

Damn shame he couldn't reach her nipples with his mouth. Those rosy peaks were made for kissing. They had puckered into hard little nubs beneath his tongue. And she liked it. A lot.

"Let me help." He brushed over the tight tips of her full breasts until she was gasping. Her hand rubbed furiously at her clit and her hips rocked back and forth. "That's it, baby, let it go. Let it go."

"Bash!" she keened as she bounced up and down for the final few strokes before collapsing into a shuddering, limp form against his chest.

"Love you," he whispered into her hair, tugging her knees up and turning her sideways until he supported her entire weight. It awed him how easily those words slipped from him as she snuggled inside his embrace.

The only thing missing was her echoing feelings. It didn't matter, though, because after a moment she lifted her chin and looked into his eyes. The answer was there, pooled in the liquid blue of her gaze.

She lifted a hand and stroked his cheek, her touch so soft. He leaned into it and squeezed his eyes shut. He never wanted this moment to end.

* * * * *

The familiar ping of a wrench hitting concrete burst through Bree's thoughts. She stood at the front of the car, waiting for Bash to tell her what he needed next. Only his jeans-clad legs stuck out from just behind the front tire, but she could tell already that something was frustrating him.

After that incredible, out-of-body experience with him in the back of his car, he'd gone quiet on her, as if their joking banter hadn't even existed. She had to be wrong in thinking the look he gave her as he dropped a kiss to her nose was apologetic.

Hell, maybe it was. Maybe he thought she'd think jumping in the back of the car was cheap or that he had come over today just to…well, come. That made her smile.

"All okay down there?"

He spit and cursed. "Dammit, no. Freaking hose is split and I just bathed in fluid."

Yikes. "Um, here." She grabbed a red garage rag and got down on the ground to pass it to him.

"Thanks."

Bathed had been the proper term. The cardboard he used as a cushion against the cold, hard concrete was saturated. His neck, the collar and shoulder of his shirt were stained. It must have hit him right on the side of the face. His hair was practically plastered to his head, all shiny with it.

"You look sticky."

He grinned. "You climb under a car and stay clean then you ain't working."

True. "Damn shame we never got around to installing a shower in here."

Silence. Bash had lifted his hands and was busy cranking on a stubborn bolt.

Was he concentrating or had she said something wrong?

Damn. She hated this. Hated it even more since they had seemed to finally get to the point where they both had accepted that they were right for one another. She never wanted anything more than she did to have Bash in her life right now. And in her bed, but that wasn't really even in question.

"Okay, I'm feeling rather helpless here. What can I do?"

He slid out from under the car. All businesslike he said, "Turn on the air compressor."

She stared at the giant blue canister for a moment, trying to remember. It's not like she'd ever used it on her own. When she'd ventured in the garage, everything was always up and running. Of course, there really wasn't a time when everything wasn't on. Not until after…

Stop it.

She flipped the switch. Light came on. Good.

Bash used his dry sleeve to wipe his eyes. Half of her wanted to laugh, the other half frown and pity his misfortune. She did neither, simply waited for her next command.

"Got any pressure?"

She grabbed the hose. It still had the small, air blower thing. Hell, she didn't know the names. All she knew was that you pulled the little trigger-like mechanism and a hard narrow burst of air shot out the end. Very good for blowing away dust and dirt.

But today, pulling the trigger did nothing. "Zilch pressure."

"Shit."

"I'm gonna go clean up. I got this crap in my eyes and mouth. It's nasty."

She bet it was. "Here," she passed over the keys.

"Come on in. I can't do much without the compressor, and I don't want you out here alone."

Right. She didn't want to be out here alone either. Despite the fact that the she'd forgotten the earlier events until he'd said that. "Right behind you."

Bash turned off the handheld light and stacked the tools in the magnetic tray. That, she recalled, had been a Christmas present Bash had gotten Luke one year from the high-end tool guy that visited them at work.

She squeezed her eyes shut, but instead of blocking out the memory, she conjured up a perfect picture. Like a video playing in her head. At least it was one of the better years.

They'd all gathered around her tabletop Christmas tree—her, Bash and Luke. It wasn't Christmas Eve— probably the night before that. She didn't care to remember. Her heart already pounded as she recalled handing Luke and Bash their gifts. She'd gotten Luke something special and intended to wait to give it to him on Christmas Day. But she'd gotten them both a gift certificate for tools, Luke's twice that of Bash's.

He'd still played hurt that their presents were the same.

Bash had leaned over and squeezed her hand, thanking her for something he didn't have to return. They all laughed, and despite Luke's moment of bitterness, their party wasn't spoiled.

Luke had given her a charm bracelet with little gold wrenches and cars and things. She'd loved it, she really had.

She wondered what had ever happened to it.

"Bree?" Bash stood at the door to the garage, watching her intently. God, it was just like that day, that Christmas. The almost hesitant way he'd handed her a tiny package.

"You didn't have to," she'd said, blushing. Luke shifted closer so he could see exactly what was in that little box. Looking back, she realized just how jealous he was, even then.

"Well, open it," Bash had said. He'd fiddled with the ribbon from an earlier package. Even now she could see his face, so boyish and nervous.

Had he really felt something for her back then? As intense as it was now?

Sparing him any further apprehension, she'd torn up the mini-reindeer paper and gasped when she saw the light blue box.

"I hope you like it."

She would. Bash had given it to her and she'd have treasured it forever. What was even better, she learned as she opened the box, was that it *was* the perfect gift.

A tiny perfume bottle that fit in the palm of her hand. The glass was cut like a crystal star. Even if it stank, she loved it.

But it didn't. It was called Angel and it smelled like heaven. It stole her breath. So refreshingly light and airy. Yet not too flowery or musky. Perfect.

Sentimental fool that she was, it awed her that he'd find her worthy of such a scent.

Luke had snorted at it and that was the end of it.

Literally.

It disappeared from her dresser within the week and she never had been able to find it again.

"Bree, you okay?"

Bash was there, right there in front of her, his palm inches from her cheek. She looked up, surprised to find her vision blurry with unshed tears. "Sorry. Just had one of those memory flashbacks."

The light in his eyes went out. "Come on. I want to get this done tonight. You need your car back for tomorrow, right?"

Damn tears. Bree wiped them away. She'd even managed to piss Bash off with them. "Right. Yeah. Sorry."

She followed him up to the house, her heart dragging on the gravel behind her.

"Help yourself to a shower," she called as he continued toward the bathroom. "I can go downstairs. I think there's a box with some old coveralls or something for you to wear while I wash your stuff."

"No thanks. I'll go home and get my own clothes."

Emphasis on *own*.

Bree stepped back, thankful Bash didn't see the stunned hurt she knew had to be reflected on her face.

Fine. Swallowing the stinging shambles of her shredded heart, she went downstairs anyway. Maybe there she could figure it out.

Had he meant it as curtly as he'd said it? Was the inflection lost because he'd yelled it halfway across the house? Without the benefit of his expression, she had no idea. Only that it'd felt like a slap in the face.

She pulled the string for the overhead light. There was nothing in the glorified cellar except a small room that held her washer and dryer and some storage boxes.

Somewhere, down in one of them, she had something Bash might agree to wear.

Determination kept her going after the overhead pipes had groaned, their way of saying Bash had finished his shower.

He'd done it dozens of times, but now there was something about him standing naked under that hot water in her house that twisted her gut. A bittersweet awareness spread through her like a wildfire.

"As if it does any good." Being good together in bed didn't make relationships work. And obviously there was still something wedged between them. She quit staring at the ceiling, lamenting her lack of X-ray vision. What she was looking for was here, and she had to find it.

"Bree?"

He was at the top of the stairs.

"Just a minute," she called. God bless it, had she packed it that well?

Yes.

She'd buried her one "piece" of Bash right after she'd learned he was gone.

"What the hell are you doing down here?" Not mean or demanding. Curious. Maybe he hadn't snapped at her earlier.

She looked up at him. Sweet mother of all that was holy and right in this world.

Why didn't she have a camera? Then she could preserve *this* moment right along with all the others she'd kept in her memories and in this box.

Bash stood at the bottom step, one hand rubbing his wet hair with a towel. Dark, wavy strands already fell rebelliously onto his forehead. He leaned against the wall with his other arm.

Damn. And men said women were curvy. Well, not like that. The muscles of his arms and shoulders were nicely defined against the dark wood of the wall behind him. His chest was wide, but not too pumped up.

Her mouth watered as her eyes traced every bump, every cleft and rippling muscle. What killed her, totally killed her, was the way his torso narrowed into slim hips that barely held onto his faded, unbuttoned jeans.

Her body went into red alert. But the sirens in her head were the result of her frantically beating heart and pounding pulse. Not to mention that the ability to breathe without conscious thought had eluded her.

"Find what you're looking for?" he asked.

"No." Probably best to give up. She'd wanted to surprise him. Heaven forbid he think she'd ignored what she was realizing was a refusal to wear anything of Luke's.

"Bree. It's August. No need to pull out the Christmas stuff."

She followed his gaze to the open box in front of her and laughed. Tension melted away. Maybe he'd just been impatient to get cleaned up. And damn did he clean up nice. Something damn sexy about a man that smelled like her. Told her he was masculine enough to use raspberry-scented shampoo.

"I'm not looking for mistletoe, silly. I didn't think I'd need it after today."

"You don't, but I already—"

She knew what he was going to say. "Hush up. I heard you."

A grin. Thank God.

But then he went and ruined it. He took a deep breath and shoved his free hand in his pocket. "Listen, Bree. About today…"

She froze. Literally went icy cold and didn't move. Couldn't. Bad news. Regrets. She didn't want to hear this.

He cleared his throat. "I think I was mistaken about earlier. About us—"

"No!" He couldn't be saying these things.

Shaking his head, he continued. "Obviously there's still a part of your heart you've reserved for Luke—"

"No!" she repeated. God no. All that was left was guilt. Pure, agonizing guilt. Every ounce of pressed down on her shoulders, pushing her from her knees into a limp sitting position on the concrete. "Wait, Bash."

"Oh, I'm not leaving. Not going anywhere at all. But perhaps we'd better back up our relationship a few steps until Luke isn't between us anymore."

Chapter Nine

This wasn't happening. The echo of Bash's steps as he ascended into the kitchen resounded in her broken heart. Even his promise not to leave failed to erase the ache. Hell, it made it worse.

Bree sniffled, then swiped angrily at the tears that defied her intentions. Dear God, she wasn't some weak sniveling crybaby who bawled her eyes out when she didn't get her way.

But today? She'd damn near gotten run over by some hedonistic maniac in a black Corvette, then…

She slammed the lid down on the rubber storage container and pulled out the next one.

…*then* she'd had the best, most heartfelt sex of her life…

Shit. Luke's trophies. Why had she kept these things? She closed the lid and pushed that one aside.

…and now the man who professed he loved her not two hours ago just put the brakes on their relationship.

Jackpot.

She pulled out the wrinkled football jersey. Damn. He'd grown. This had fit him from junior year in high school until well, until he'd left.

He'd taken to wearing it in the garage, evidenced by the grease stains permanently darkening a couple of spots on the shoulders. She remembered the last time she'd seen him in it. Their first night. He'd yanked it over his head and tossed it on top of her clothes.

When he'd left, she'd gotten him a clean shirt—Bash had always kept spare clothes at the house back then—and promised to wash the jersey.

She pulled the sleek material closer and sniffed. At least it wasn't musty. But then again, she'd put it away after finally giving in and washing it. She'd hid it here, in her laundry room for weeks, pulling it out every once in a while to smell Bash's lingering scent on it.

Snapping the lid on that box, she fisted the shirt and smiled. She wasn't bothering to restack those boxes. They could wait.

Bash couldn't.

"Bash?" she called, taking the steps two at a time.

By the time she got to the top, the unease had returned. After all, she wasn't completely sure what had set him off. The bit about borrowing an old bit of clothing had merely pushed him over the edge. What had started it? Did he regret making love to her?

She found him standing at the living room window, staring through the half-turned blinds. A shiver raced up her back. *The car.*

"Is...I-is he—"

"No." He approached her, his face blank.

That hurt. It was as if he'd emptied out all his emotion. How could he?

"I'm going to run out and see about getting a new hose. Hopefully I can get it to stop leaking today, since that seems to be the main culprit. Pump does need to be changed, though, I'm just not going to be able to finish it all tonight."

Basically he'd just said, "I'm out of here".

"Here." Dammit. Her voice shook. So did her hand as she passed over the shirt.

"What?"

She turned away, his almost cruel question like a slap. "A piece of history, Sebastian. Your history."

Taking the coward's way out, she fled to her bedroom.

* * * * *

Bash knew immediately what she handed him. The telltale material and shade of light blue could be nothing else.

His jersey. *His.* Not Luke's.

He'd forgotten he'd left it here. Shit, how could he forget? He'd gone to sleep that night imagining her wearing it to bed, her scent mingling with his. Her cute, upturned breasts would push against the material, stroking those nipples the way he longed to. She'd wear nothing beneath. He could just picture her standing there, that dark blonde thatch of hair between her legs not quite hidden beneath the hem of the shirt.

He tightened wondering if she *had* worn it, but forced himself not to lift it to his nose.

When he'd left her that day, both of them a little confused and completely unsure of where things would go next, he'd found something in her eyes he had never seen again in anyone else.

Bliss. Unadulterated love. Satisfaction. How ironic.

Yet he could have sworn he'd seen glimpses if it today, too. Guess that's what his problem was, he'd actually thought she'd pushed Luke and his memories behind her and could give him everything she'd promised two years ago.

Well, maybe *she* hadn't promised, but those wells of blue she called eyes certainly had.

Then she'd gone and teared up over some melancholy memory of Luke.

If that hadn't been enough, she'd had the audacity to offer him some of *his* clothes. Granted, she was trying to be nice, but…

He held the jersey up and looked at it again. There was probably some message here that any female would immediately recognize. Damned if he knew what it was.

Was she giving it back? Admitting she'd treasured it for years? Kept it safe for him? Regardless, it wasn't going to fit him now.

So now what? He tossed the shirt over his shoulder and massaged his temples. Probably should go after her. But then what?

Apologize? What did he do wrong?

Women. He needed a damn translator.

* * * * *

Much as he hated to do it, he slipped back into his sticky T-shirt and went back out to the garage. Maybe he'd figure out what he needed to do while he was out there. With Bree. He knew exactly what the car needed.

The humid air of the garage engulfed him in what he and Luke had called pressurized hell. Breathing was damn near impossible and sweat broke out on his body immediately. He kicked on the fans they'd mounted up in the corners and waited until the air started circulating.

Maybe it was his imagination, but he could almost smell the musky hint of sex mixed with the ever-present scent of oil and gas.

He stepped closer to his car. Hell, yeah. His interior had clenched that scent and tortured him with it.

Bree was right there, miserable as he was. All he had to do was walk back across the driveway and wrap her into his arms. He had little doubt she'd be willing to indulge him physically.

"Fuck!" He kicked the tire of the Chevy. "Damn you, Luke, Damn you for destroying the last chance I have to—"

"Who are you talking to?"

Like an angel, she stood in the doorway. The sunlight lit up her hair, turning it into a golden halo. But it also hid her features in shadow.

"No one," he answered, mentally kicking the tire one last time.

"No one?" But I heard you. Sounded like—"

"I was venting." Now or never. He walked up to her and put his hands on her shoulders. "As long as I'm blaming Luke or you're thinking of him or either of us shelters an ounce of guilt, we're doomed."

Those precious pink lips tightened into a narrow line. "You're right."

"So, what are we going to do?" He looked around, then back at her. How could she be right here...in his arms, yet he couldn't have her, at least not the way he wanted.

She shrugged, her eyes clouded. After blinking a few times, she forced a smile and said, "Fix my car."

He groaned as she walked past him and tore a poster off the wall. "While I do some housekeeping."

"Bree, wait—" What the hell was she doing?

"Wait for what?" She turned, that sad, sad smile ripping his gut wide open. "Another two years? It's my garage, Bash. I can do whatever I please."

"Don't do it on my account."

He felt her pain, her confusion. He should just shut up and let her exorcise her demons any way she wanted.

"I'm doing this on *my* account. I'm not letting a dead man dictate my life two years after I—"

"Son of a bitch," Bash roared and raced out of the garage.

Couldn't this-this motherfucker leave them alone for a day? It was as if it was listening and appearing when the *last* thing Bree needed was more confusion.

This car wasn't trying to kill him, or Bree. *He* was trying to slaughter any chance of a relationship between them. A fate worse than death.

"Bash!"

"Get back inside. Now. Don't get in the middle of this."

She didn't move. Instead, stood beside him with arms crossed over her chest and knees locked. "Too late for that. Tell me what the hell this is all about."

Her voice wavered. Her eyes shifted from him to the car. Brave girl, he had to give her credit. But she was way out of her league here. Didn't stand a chance.

The 'vette crouched at the end of the driveway, rocking back and forth as the powerful engine roared at them. Bash wasn't sure it wouldn't strike.

"It's not too late. Go." He'd face his adversary another time. Right now he had to think of Bree. Grabbing her arm, he pulled her toward the garage door and pushed her in ahead of him. As he slammed the door, he heard the Corvette burp the throttle, as if laughing at him, and then roared off up the street.

God*damn* it. Were they always going to be caught in this endless loop? He'd never be able to escape the car, or Bree's questions. He'd gone and accused her of holding Luke between them and he had a bigger issue than that.

And a secret he hadn't come close to admitting to her.

"We need to talk." He yanked on the doorknob after double-checking the lock.

"Damn straight." Her fear had smoldered into anger. Her face was flame red, and her temper matched. "What *is* that thing?" She shook a forefinger at the large bay door. "Or better yet, *who* is that?"

"It's not Luke." Best to stop that train of thought before it left the station. "I swear it."

He walked toward her, anxious to close the gap, both physically and emotionally. Both of them needed to relax and understand that they both wanted the same thing.

Bree shook her head. "Luke's dead. I buried him. I helped his mother choose a casket and pick out the funeral music. I saw his body—his injuries. I know it's not him. Alive, anyway."

He wished he could have been there, comforting her, taking on those responsibilities that no one should have to face at such a tender age. But he couldn't.

"You're right, he's dead. He's gone. This isn't about Luke at all."

Her sigh meant she wasn't accepting that statement.

"You and I," he continued before there was another interruption. "We have Luke issues. But that's not his fault. You have to let go of any guilt associated with being with me. We are single adults. It's not cheating if your fiancé is dead." Harsh, but true. Still, he winced at the raw emotion that clouded her eyes.

"I didn't say…"

"It's not in your words. But that doesn't even matter. We should have addressed this earlier. I want you in my life, Bree. There's no game in that. I don't even think you question that, do you?"

She shook her head.

Good. Too bad it wasn't all that simple. He was beginning to wonder if happily ever after existed only in fairy tales. "The car." He stopped and took a deep breath. He should just blurt it out. But no, not when there was still fear lurking in those gentle features. Not when he knew without a doubt he'd break her heart yet again with his news. Clearing his throat he continued, "The car is getting more aggressive—"

"Wait. Why do you call it 'the car' and not by the driver's name? Or just say, 'he' or whatever?"

"I worry about you, here alone like this. I don't know what he wants with you. Or what he'll do."

"You never answered my question. I deserve to know. Who—or what—is stalking me, you or anyone who tries to get near us—"

"Who?" His chest tightened. "What are you talking about?"

Bree related the cop story. All the while he clenched and unclenched his jaw, tightening his fists until he thought his fingers would break. Oh, he knew it was just a scare tactic and the cop wasn't really in any danger. But Bree didn't know that. He had to wonder. Was she bait?

He couldn't take the chance.

"Dammit." This time he pulled her stiff body into his arms and hugged her tight until she finally relaxed. "I'm staying here with you from now on."

She gasped.

"I'll sleep in the guest room, on the couch, even here in the garage. Wouldn't be the first time. I'm not leaving here, leaving you alone." He cupped her head and tilted until she lifted her eyes to his. "But you know where I want to sleep."

She tore her gaze from his and wriggled.

"I won't let him get to you. To us."

"I don't need a damn babysitter."

"Were you not paying attention to what you just told me? The car is coming here when I'm not around. Threatening other people. Like I said. I'm staying. You have no choice."

That was *not* the right answer. Bree tore out of his arms and stomped back into the house.

What the hell was she doing now? Reacting. Badly. It was overwhelming. Of course she wanted him to stay—hadn't that been exactly what she'd mentally pleaded for last night?

Without Bash here, regardless of what room he chose, sleep for her would be as elusive as a—

"Hemi in a Chevy."

The line Luke used to say. She pushed her fists against her eye sockets and rubbed. How could she be thinking of the fringe benefits of having Bash move in while Luke's voice was still in her head, finishing her thoughts?

Wait a minute.

Her entire body shook. Goose bumps popped out of every bit of exposed skin.

She pushed her hair out of her face and slowly opened her eyes. No way would she stake money on her coming up with that phrase all on her own.

"Luke?" Barely a whisper, but enough to make her blood run cold.

He was here. Madness, tears, anger, fear, guilt—it all welled up into a peal of hysterical laughter.

Ridiculous. Now she was *talking* to air. Of course Luke wasn't here. And surely if he were he'd be doing everything he could to scare her—and scare Bash away.

She headed to her bedroom. Maybe dunking her head under some cold water would clear out those crazy thoughts and make her capable of getting her shit together.

As she walked, she forced her thoughts to Bash. Damn him for pulling the upper hand and pissing her off. Right when she thought they'd gotten on the same page about this mess.

What he'd said—about it not being her choice—sounded just like something Luke would have said.

Luke. Bash. A sinister ghost car and her own wicked imagination. Love. Guilt. Where did all the pieces of this puzzle fit?

She flipped on the hallway light, ducking and whimpering as one of the bulbs popped. Then she giggled at herself. This however, was evidence to what she was dealing with. The events of the last three days had her gun-shy — everything shy, really.

Piece of cake, Bree. Bulbs and stepstool in the hall closet. Nothing to freak out over. See?

Or, she could go get Bash.

She stared at the simple, white light cover. *No.* She didn't need Bash for this one. Had it gone out last week she wouldn't have even *thought* about how unfortunate it was she didn't have a man around it change it.

Not that she didn't want Bash around. She wanted him. Didn't need him. Of that she was confident.

Straightening her spine, she yanked open the closet door.

And let out a bloodcurdling scream.

Bash raced up the steps and through the house. That shriek had ripped inside him and grabbed hold of his heart and lungs and rendered them unusable.

There was no reason for her to be afraid. The car had left. He'd have heard it if it had returned.

Maybe she fell.

Hell, maybe there was a spider on the ceiling.

He doubted it. There was an icy terror in the way it had carried across the yard. And he couldn't get to her fast enough.

"Bree, where are you?"

Hallway light was on. He turned the corner just as he heard her sob.

"What?"

The closet door was open, blocking his view of her. "What?" he asked again, pulling the door farther, then gasping as he saw what she had.

First shock, then hurt, and finally anger took turns twisting his gut. Closing his eyes, counting to three and then opening them again didn't take away the destruction he found there.

"What happened?"

"Get away from me. How could you? Dammit!" She threw something at him. It bounced harmlessly off his chest. When it fell at his feet, recognition registered. Luke's favorite leather racing jacket, the arm of it at least. It was destroyed.

Her accusation floored him. He couldn't even defend himself, for the shock of it. Yet, already there it was, whatever monster had taken a straight edge to every piece of clothing in the closet that had once been Luke's now carved a hole of guilt in him. If he hadn't come back, if he hadn't gotten involved with Bree, this wouldn't have happened.

Wasn't he guilty by proxy?

"You didn't do this? When—? How—?" It floored him that someone could come in the house without any other sign of an intruder and do something like this. "When was the last time you were in here?"

"You think I'd do this? Destroy these?"

Never mind that it hurt like hell that she still kept so many treasures of her fiancé around. But he had to know this. "Why did you have them? Why were these in here?"

"I couldn't throw them away. I've always intended to give them to charity." Her lips were set in a tight line, the skin surrounding them white with effort. "You," she started, pointing right at his chest. "You were the only one with access to this closet. No one has been in the house for...months."

That she knew of.

"I didn't do it. Hell yeah, I want you to quit thinking of him, of feeling guilty that I'm here and you're happy about it. Do you think I'd take the chance of pissing you off like that?" He gestured at the mess. Two racing ball caps had been sliced into pieces, none of the remains bigger than his hand. From the heap of leather and denim on the ground, he'd guessed she must have had two or three jackets in there. Everything in shambles.

"What if..." She closed her eyes and sucked in two deep breaths. "What if I told you to leave and that I never wanted to see you again. Would all this go away?"

"Only I would. The car? It might come back, it might not. I can't say, Brehann." He put his hands on her shoulders and waited until she lifted her face. How could she even suggest such a thing? "But do you really want me to go?" Leaning forward, he ran his hands down her arms and then back up again, memorizing everything he could about her in case she said yes. "I swear on my grave that I didn't do this."

Her eyes grew wide. Pushing his hands away, she shivered. God, how he wanted to bundle her up in the front of his car and drive—miles from here. But the horror would follow, it always did. And he wondered if the car was really the biggest problem they were facing after all.

Bree knew there wasn't an easy answer, if indeed there was one.

She stared at him, then the horror in the closet, even her own hands, then back again. In the end, she blamed common sense on influencing her.

"What time it is?"

"Nearly six," he said, glancing at his watch.

"Okay. Here's the deal. I'm calling Smitty's for pizza delivery. Then you're going to go play garage until bed. You'll sleep in the guest room. If you need to get clothes from your house, go now, while it's still light. I'll clean up here and do whatever."

He sighed in relief. There was no sign of disappointment that she had given him separate sleeping quarters.

"One more thing."

"Anything."

She blinked. Then gave in and smiled. Deep down in her heart, she knew he hadn't been the one to destroy the clothes. His face had mirrored the shock and pain she'd felt. She'd lashed out from exhaustion and shock and hurt. Probably the way he had when he'd ordered her around in the garage, all fired up about the damn car returning. What a fucked-up mess. "Crap, I don't remember."

He laughed then, full bodied and rich. It poured over and around her with the effects of brandy—warm and intoxicating. And just like the drink, it was felt the most right in the center of her chest.

"Go, get. Before I change my mind." It was more of a tease now, and she was sure he knew it, but he still didn't argue. She bit her bottom lip and watched him.

He was still laughing as he walked away.

But then she looked down. The sight was nothing less than a bucket of icy water on her. Someone had done this. It wasn't her imagination.

The "who" scared her more than "why".

She just prayed having Bash here in the house wasn't inviting more trouble.

* * * * *

This was the stupidest idea she had come up with yet. It drove her nuts to have him in the house with her with the hands-off terms she'd suggested. And dammit, she wasn't even mad at him — really hadn't been. So why were they circling each other like two lions ready to pounce?

"You gonna eat any more of that pizza?"

Bree tried not to stare at the perfect picture Bash made there on the couch. He'd discarded his shirt over an hour before and now lay on his side, half hugging the pillow as he watched some forensic detective show on TV.

"Nah, I'm done."

She snatched it up and carried it to the kitchen. What a fool she was. This wasn't the tenth grade anymore. She couldn't just stand around and wait for Bash to make a move. Not when *she'd* been the dunce who'd set the limitations. Separate bedrooms. Ha. She'd expected him to put up a little resistance. But no, he'd driven off somewhere and returned with a duffel bag full of supplies and moved right into the guest room. It was a game now, she guessed. And she wasn't very good at playing. He, however, seemed to have no problem with it.

Nope. Looks like if she wanted anything else out of tonight, she'd have to go for it herself.

What if he said no?

He wouldn't say no. They'd already had sex—just this afternoon.

Which means he could say no and it wouldn't really be a strain on his system.

He's a man. We've admitted how we feel about each other.

And recognized there are some serious flaws in this relationship.

Grr. She twisted the tap and started washing the plates. She put them away when she realized she was darn near scrubbing the pattern off.

What was she trying to erase? The past? Her fear? She glanced at the doorway that led to the living room. The light from the TV flashed against the dividing wall. What would it be like to live like this? Would she ever be able to do so without the fear of losing him the way—

Her fists pounded on the counter.

That's what she wanted to erase. Those thoughts. Those…memories.

"Bree?"

He was there, at the corner.

She blinked back tears and smiled. "Sorry."

"What's going on?" He looked around, his eyes half closed, probably from the bright overhead light. Hell, he might have even fallen asleep in there. His hair was tousled, his one cheek a little pink from being pressed against the pillow. Beautiful. How could her heart not explode in her chest looking at that?

"Just, uh, doing dishes."

"Oh. Thought I heard banging."

Just my head against the wall for being so stupid. "It was nothing. Sorry. You ready for bed?" That's not what her mouth was supposed to say. She was intending on something a little more...hell, direct, like "Take me to bed".

"When you are."

Was she supposed to read that as, "I'm joining you," or was it simply the whole formal hostess/guest thing that she was overanalyzing?

She nodded. "It's been a long day." Too long. Seemed like days, not hours ago that they'd eaten lunch.

Do it, you moron.

"Uh, Bash?"

She might *know* that she wasn't in high school anymore, but her body was reacting as if she was. Her stomach twisted, her hands dampened and her knees threatened to collapse under her weight.

"Yeah?"

"I-I..."

Screw it.

She walked up to him, threw her arms around his neck and pressed her lips to his.

He stood there, so solid and unmoving for a second she just knew it was a mistake. All wrong. What a fool.

She was ready to apologize when his hands crept up on her hips and nudged her a little closer to his body. Close enough that she could feel the heat coming off his bare chest.

Whimpering, she threaded her fingers in his hair and angled her mouth, opening to his probing tongue, welcoming the moist, velvety heat inside her. Making him part of her.

She shattered.

Fell apart, weak with the relief that he wouldn't deny her.

Holding him for dear life, she kissed and cried, tasting the salty tang of her tears and feeling the way he held her, cherished her, stroking her back and cradling her head.

Suddenly she was weightless, still carefully folded into the cocoon of his arms. He carried her. She didn't care where, just knew she was ripped in two by the wanting, and the fear of losing.

The cool sheets were unwelcome. She reached out in the darkness as his hands slid away from her body. He was so far away. Fading…fading as the exhaustion claimed her.

No! Don't leave.

The covers were pulled up over her shoulders tucked around her. His breath tickled her ear as he leaned down and pressed a kiss to her temple. "Sleep, precious. I'll be here. Tomorrow it'll all be better."

It would? She was so tired. So…pulled in so many directions. But she knew she didn't want Bash to leave. The room or her house or her life. Ever.

"I love you," she whispered, unsure if he heard her or not.

Chapter Ten

Bash sat back on the couch and stared into the night.

He'd seen it coming. It'd been his fault. Everything had gone so fast, had run hot and cold all damn day — until *he* wasn't sure where they were and what level they were on. He was surprised she'd been able to make it as long as she did. Then she'd thrown herself at him and fallen apart. Damn, what was he supposed to do then? No way was he taking advantage, despite his body's immediate reaction. But she hadn't fought him when he'd carried her to bed, and had been asleep when he'd left the room. Poor thing. Damn strong woman for making it this far. Hopefully a good night's sleep would help her recover.

At least that damn car hadn't returned and fucked their world up a little more.

He was beginning to think that Bree's half-serious suggestion that Luke was back, haunting her, wasn't so off the mark.

He scratched his head. God. Could he seriously be contemplating that? If so, what message would he have ventured from the grave to try to deliver?

"Christ." He was losing it. Probably should check the perimeter and head to bed himself. Not that he wouldn't just lay there and imagine he could hear her breathing down the hall, imagining what it'd be like to spoon against her perfect little ass and bury his head into the nape of her neck.

His cock twitched and hardened. Another bit of proof that he was in no shape to be awake. He'd felt protective and concerned when he'd put her into bed and now he was thinking about waking her up and…

Tomorrow. They'd figure it out. And maybe then put some definition to their relationship.

Instead of simply locking the back door, Bash ventured outside and closed it behind him gently, then stood there. The air around him still held some of the humidity of the day, but the temperature had dropped. Perfect weather. Stars above twinkled, leaves rustled with the breeze. He'd love nothing more than to sit here, beside Bree, of course, and spend every night like this before heading off to bed.

The quiet was strange, though. His mind was still struggling to escape from the deep ruts of his memory, when he couldn't walk out of the house without hearing the loud music and see the garage ablaze with light, all the doors open in hopes some cool air would circulate through. Even the air smelled differently now—so clean and earthy. The tang of oil and gas had faded.

New chapter. He nodded and set out to check the garage. New chapter indeed.

Halfway there, he stopped. He closed his eyes and held his breath, feeling his skin crawl, the hairs on the back of his neck rising.

Someone was out there. He'd heard something, maybe even sensed something. He waited.

There.

A crunch on the gravel.

A footstep.

"Who's there?" Opening his eyes he spun around, expecting to see the outline of a person somewhere within the range of the porch light. It wasn't a very dark night anyway. He could make out silhouettes of trees and even her mailbox there at the end of the driveway.

Whoever it was, was hiding.

Or his imagination had run wild and he was startled by a squirrel racing across the drive.

Regardless, he shivered and picked up his pace, practically jogging the rest of the distance to the garage.

"You can't change what's supposed to happen, you know."

Bash froze, one hand on the garage door. An icy cold finger of fear traced its way down his back, freezing his blood and numbing his senses. He knew that voice. Thinking his name raised the goose bumps on his flesh.

"Luke?" he could barely force his breath out to speak.

"You're a fool, Bernecchi."

He whirled. He was right there, right behind him. But when he turned, nothing.

Nothing.

Bash used both hands to push the hair off his face, blinked and then rubbed his eyes and squinted into the darkness. Why couldn't he see him? Was it his imagination?

"A fool."

Bash glanced over at Bree's window. Still dark, no sign of movement. "Show yourself," he said to the man who spoke to him.

Deep laughter filled the air, echoing off the side of the building. Bash tensed, eyes never leaving that window. The light glinted off the glass. He knew it was open. If she were awake, she could have heard that. And then she would know.

"Catch you off balance, did I, buddy?"

Friend or foe? Bash couldn't understand why Luke spoke in riddles and hid himself. "Why? Why are you here? Why'd you come back? What unfinished business do you have?"

"You've no reason to be here," Luke countered.

"She's my reason. You know that." Bash turned, unable to see him, but knew he circled him, sizing him up. "What's your reason?"

"I came back for you."

"I'm not going." Crossing his arms over his chest did little good, he knew, but he was standing his ground in any way he could. "I'm not ready."

"Fate doesn't go by your schedule. You're late."

The voice faded. No sooner could Bash turn around and run for the porch than the car was in the driveway, bright lights blinding him. Gravel flew up, punctuating the roar of eight angry cylinders.

Above it all, he heard Bree scream.

Bash!

She jumped out of bed, feet tangling in the comforter and nearly tripping her. *No! He can't leave!*

She jerked the blinds open. Then gasped.

It was back. The car. The light glared off the window, preventing her from seeing much more than the silhouette of the nose and fender. That, coupled with the roar she should have known wasn't Bash's '55, made her one hundred percent sure of what she was seeing.

It was back. After her.

Why?

Why?

A figure crossed in front of the headlights. Still the engine raced.

"Bash!" she screamed. Or tried to. It came out in a painful croak.

Where was he? Still in bed? Surely he heard this. He had to.

The back door slammed.

Shit.

Weapon. *Come on, Bree. Think.* Last thing she needed to do was turn on a light or make noise and lead whoever it was straight to her. Where the hell was Bash? Hopefully he was out there confronting him.

Ducking into the master bathroom, she grabbed the wooden-handled toilet brush. Best case scenario, she could stun the intruder and run out to the neighbors and call 9-1-1. Or wake up Bash. Or…

She braced herself near the bedroom door, brush held over her head. God. What if she missed? Her already uneasy stomach twisted into another knot of dread.

Heavy footsteps echoed in the hall. Bash wouldn't stomp through like that. He'd call out, wouldn't he? Ask if she were up. Check to be sure she was okay.

No, this man was after her—coming straight for her room.

Then time stuttered. It was all in slow motion.

There was no light, yet she swore she could see the door handle turning. Likely too many suspense movies.

Her knees shook, her arms tingled from being held up above her head for so long. She breathed slow and shallow while her lungs screamed for oxygen. The element of surprise was on her side. *Don't blow it.*

Just as the door opened, she swung down, as hard as she could.

Too late.

Recognition couldn't stop the momentum of her arms.

The handle hit Bash squarely on the top of the head, sending him crashing to the bedroom floor.

She dropped to her knees beside him. "Bash, I'm so sorry. I thought—"

"Bree."

"I'm here. Oh God. Are you okay?" The connection had been solid. Her arms still reverberated from the impact.

He groaned and rolled to his side, clutching his head in his hands.

Outside, the car thundered like an impending storm.

She swallowed and looked up toward the window. What was going on here? Who had been outside? *Bash?* Why?

"What the hell was that for?" he muttered. He sat up, then laid back down. "And what the hell did you hit me with?"

"You were outside."

He didn't answer, just grabbed her wrist.

"Ow!" She tried to jerk from the fingers that cut into the flesh there. "What?"

"I can't—we can't…"

This time she pried his fingers off her arm and stood to turn on the light.

He was fully dressed. Probably had never gotten undressed. That sickened her heart. It was too hard not to wonder if he was behind this after all.

"We can't what?" She dropped back to her knees, so sorry she'd hurt him, but slightly tempted to take her makeshift weapon and threaten him until he spit out the answers.

"You and me. That's why it's here. Dammit."

She helped him sit up, hating the lines of pain on his handsome face. Gently, she pulled his fingers away from the point of impact.

No blood, thank God. Just a nicely raised ridge that extended halfway down his forehead.

"Cute," she said, grimacing. "You've got some prehistoric, bony-type Mohawk going on there."

He moaned.

"Do you want me to call an ambulance? Or I can drive you to—shit. No, I can't. We didn't get my car fixed."

"No. No doctors. Just go…lock up. God, that hurts." Felt like he'd head-butted the side of the *Titanic*. The fact that his eyes didn't want to focus just intensified the pain.

"You might have a concussion."

Minor compared to what he'd visited the hospital with last time. Besides, all hell would literally break loose when they went to punch his name into the computer there. He hadn't quite got around to explaining all that to

Bree yet. So no, abso-fucking-lutely no hospital for him. "Just help me into bed."

Just like that, no argument, nothing. So far, so good.

Until she put her hands under his arms and tried to lift.

He laughed, or started to. The effort throbbed through his temples.

"I can't pick you up."

No kidding. "Give me a minute then. Go lock up. Make sure the car's gone." Had it left? His memory was foggy.

Bree's cool hands felt good on his cheeks and smoothing his forehead—just as long as she didn't graze that tender spot right up the middle.

In fact, her touch was just what he needed. "Wait," he said, keeping his eyes closed. She'd stopped touching him, but she hadn't left. "Never mind the car, or the door. It won't keep him out anyway."

Her fingers slowly stroked his jaw. He blocked out everything but the sensation she gave him—cold chills over every inch of flesh.

"I really am sorry," she whispered, her breath on his skin tingling even more than her touch. "I can't believe I hit you."

He swallowed. "What did you intend to hit?"

He watched her now, the sharpness of the pain receding, leaving just the dull throb that faded with her continued ministrations.

"I don't know—I looked..." She glanced toward the window and then twisted her hands. "At first I thought you were leaving. I heard the car."

"I told you—"

"I know. I woke up out of a dead sleep and that was the first thing that ran through my head. But when I looked out the window, I saw the car. And someone walking in front of the headlights."

He winced at her choice of words. After he heard *dead* sleep the rest of her explanation blurred into nothing. "Huh?" he asked. But she didn't respond. Her attention was on the window.

"I'll be right back."

She darted out of the room. Though he couldn't hear it from here, he knew she had flipped the deadbolt on the door and extinguished the lights in the house. He should tell her. Right now. Especially after what—who—he'd experienced today. It was only a matter of time before Luke spoke, or appeared to her. What if Luke beat him to telling her the truth?

"Come here," he said, dreading every second of this. He couldn't get up to follow her, or even pull himself up on the bed. Moving too quickly made him dizzy. Yet it had to be done. Sooner or later.

She did. He pulled her down sideways into his lap and waited for her to relax. And for the wave of pain to dissipate. Damn, had she done a number on him. What the hell had she used, a sledgehammer?

"Tell me what you saw outside. Just the car?"

"Now? No, it's gone."

He nodded. Just slightly. "Earlier. You said you looked out the window?" Had she seen him, talking to air? Hell, maybe Luke was visible to her and not to him. Already he knew the Corvette was invisible—and silent—to damn near everyone but himself and Bree.

Something Luke had said nagged at him. As Bree explained how she'd seen a figure walk across the yard and pass in front of the lights, he tried to remember Luke's exact words. Wasn't it about being able to change things? As in future things?

Was he saying, indirectly, that Bree's life was in danger? Did he know something that was going to take place in the future? Did Luke think he was there to prevent it? Sure sounded like it.

"Why were you outside, anyway?" she asked.

He shrugged, pulling his focus back on the wonderful, warm, *live* body on his lap. "Locking up. Making sure I'd locked up the garage." *Getting fresh air to clear my head and erase thoughts of climbing into bed with you instead of that cold spare bed where I'd said I'd sleep.*

Even now, the idea of curling up around her body and feeling its warmth all night long had his cock tightening against his jeans.

"Bree?"

"Hmm?"

"I'm feeling a little better. I've got an idea about what will make me forget about the pain." *And Luke's cryptic words.*

She shifted, as if answering that she knew exactly what he was talking about. That sweet pressure of her perfect little ass against his erection was certainly commanding all current and future thought processes. To hell with the damn car. Let it threaten them. He had Bree.

"What's that, hon?" she asked, finally sitting still.

He wanted to grip her hips and pull her back so he could grind against the crease of her ass until he came. But that's what she expected. "I'm feeling a bit short of breath. Maybe you should give me some mouth to mouth."

Bree laughed.

He groaned as her body vibrated against him. "Hold still, dammit."

Naturally, she giggled again. He swore under his breath. Damn woman was going to be the death of him. "Thought you wanted to help me here. I think you're trying to kill me. At least torture me some more."

"Oh yeah?"

"Yeah. You're supposed to be making it up to me for clobbering me with... You never did say what kind of weapon you used."

Would the woman never stop laughing? It wasn't going to be funny when he shot his load all over her ass— through their clothes.

"What?" he asked, getting exasperated that he was somehow being left out of this joke.

Then he followed the direction of her pointing fingers. No. No fucking way. What was he doing so—knocked out after being assaulted with a-a-a— "Tell me that's not what I think it is."

"Toilet brush."

"Shit." She was just adding to his injury.

She threw her head back and laughed, practically bouncing up and down on his painfully hard cock, while exposing her creamy neck to him. Was he ever going to survive this?

He reached for a nibble of that tempting flesh. As soon as his lips touched her, she stilled, then shuddered. A-ha. So she wasn't unaffected.

"So, did you expect to humiliate him when you whacked him with the brush?" He made sure his lips vibrated against her skin as he tasted and questioned her. Control was barely held in check, but this vixen needed a taste of her own teasing medicine.

"Just, uh, stun him. S-so I could find you."

"And here I was thinking you were leaving me to deal with him all by myself. After all, you didn't stock my room with such potent weaponry." He nibbled at the base of her neck, biting gently so as not to leave marks. But dammit, he wanted marks, all over her. Marks that screamed she was his possession.

"I think you're big and bad enough to handle it."

She rose up off his lap and turned around. As she sat down again, she slipped her hand to cover his zipper and squeezed. Fuck. The way she rubbed made him wonder if she was reaffirming just how big and bad he really was.

He tightened his muscles, trying to ignore the way her fingers pushed just enough against the strained denim to mimic the tight strokes of her velvety walls when he was inside her. And dammit, what he wouldn't give to have her in this position with no clothes on. God, he could bury his cock so far inside her... He moaned just imagining.

"How's the head?"

His fingers fisted in the carpet as she rubbed over the tip of his cock. She had to know what she was doing. What was that about getting even? Somehow she'd snagged the upper hand again. "Head? Mmm. Head's fine." Way fine. Ready to explode fine.

"Silly. Not this head." She squeezed.

He damn near erupted.

"This head." She touched his forehead with her free hand.

Who cared a shit about that head when her hand was busy encouraging every drop of blood in his body to rush toward his groin? "Whatever."

Enough of that. He'd come in here with a shred of hope of seducing her and she was mauling him. He knocked her hand out of the way and pulled her closer. What he could do without those damn clothes in the way.

God, she was beautiful.

The only light was the small bedside lamp. It was dim, and he could almost imagine it cast the same yellow haze a room full of candles would. Yet he wished it were brighter so he could capture every detail of her mussed hair and flushed face in his effort to commit it to memory.

He kissed her then, nudging her face closer with pressure on the back of her neck. Sweet. Somehow innocent, yet enough to set his blood on fire.

When she pulled back to catch her breath, her eyes sparkled beneath heavy lids and her lips glistened with the moisture of his kiss. Her tongue darted out, swiping over her bottom lip. He nearly lost it then.

"What are you thinking?" he asked, stroking the pad of his thumb over the silkiness of her cheek. The spell around them seemed so fragile. He was terrified to move too fast and shatter it.

"I'm afraid, Bash." She bit her lip and then held her eyes closed for a moment. When she opened them, he saw deep into them to the turmoil in her heart. "I just know. I can feel it. You won't stay. You...can't."

"Bree, I—"

"Shut up and kiss me. Make me forget that fear. Make me believe I'm never going to lose you. After all this, I can't bear to lose you."

He groaned, this time from the ache of the tear in his heart. She was right, of course. Didn't know how she'd come to this conclusion right here, right now, but she was right. That was the problem. There was no way he could stay as long as she'd need him. So he kissed her instead.

While the sensation of her mouth against his numbed the ache and temporarily erased the doubts, he knew they'd linger and eventually the truth would have to come out.

But not tonight. Not when the beauty of their lovemaking was yet to come, when they had all night to explore and be with one another. He'd give her something to remember.

Bree wanted to cry. One minute she'd been laughing, toying with Bash—on her bedroom floor no less, eager for the next step—a round of playful, exhilarating sex. But then he'd gone and kissed her in a way that was too much like good-bye. That she couldn't take.

Yet it'd been there from the beginning, this doubt. It'd all been too coincidental, the day he'd returned, the car that seemed to insist on following and intimidating them. That car, that driver, was after Bash. She'd seen it in the way it'd jumped at him when he darted across, as if teasing him, threatening to run him over. After her, too, but so strange it hadn't come around until Bash had. Maybe it was using her—threatening her to get to Bash.

She'd just denied these bits of truth. Tried to, at least. But something in the way Bash was acting tonight, the *desperation* she saw in his eyes... God, it sucked to be right.

His fingers cradled her face with such reverence.

She opened her eyes to his and acknowledged him with a slight nod. Eyes as dark as midnight implored hers, then softened as he leaned into her. His lips brushed hers, his tongue pressing between them, stroking the fullness that swelled in her chest. It was love, pure love in the way his mouth stopped and swept gentle kisses at the corners of her lips, then her cheeks, her eyes... It stole her breath. There could be nothing better than this, yet it ached. Ached in knowing that this couldn't be forever. Her heart splintered into a zillion pieces.

Bash didn't stop his exploration and she didn't want him to. She needed this, wanted him so badly to deny she was right, yet she'd seen it in his eyes. His own pain, longing and love—little comfort. But at least they had now.

Closing her eyes, she concentrated on the way his fingers left a tidal wave of tingling nerve endings as he explored her neck and throat. His face was shadowy in the dim light, but the look she saw was full of concentration...and sadness.

No way would she stop him. Or hurry him. Words weren't necessary.

She pushed an errant lock of hair away from his creased forehead, then traced the lines there. It seemed she could feel the mirroring touch in her soul. Even he stilled, his hands still hot against her flesh as they waited, neither wanting the moment to pass.

Such a mystery, her heart was so full, yet so broken. Everything to do with Bash was a mystery.

She reached for him. Dark, thick waves engulfed her fingers. Like liquid silk, his hair poured over her hands as she pulled his mouth back to hers for a deeper, more desperate kiss.

What started slow quickly built to a heated level of need. Lifting her head only when she needed to breathe, Bree marveled at the way the strokes of Bash's tongue against hers seemed to echo through her body and send electrical shocks from her labia and clit, as if his mouth were there, providing the same attentions.

Eager for more, afraid to let the tension fade, she angled her mouth over his and opened her mouth to him, tangling her tongue with his, stoking up a fire that she never wanted to quench.

Her fingers slid from his hair and roamed his face. The light scratch of stubble against her palms sent another wave of tingling sensations over her entire body, like hot-cold chills. Her nipples tightened as she imagined his mouth and face scraping over that sensitive skin, knowing she'd experience it very soon.

Bash shifted, forcing his cock to push against the material of his jeans and rub against her pants. The friction there tore a moan from her, the pressure on her clit nearly forcing her to grind against him until she found release.

But then his hands slipped up under her shirt and grazed the bottom of her breast. She gasped, holding his shoulders as he teased the skin there through the thin lace of her bra. They responded to his touch by swelling and pressing against the material, the nipples so tight they hurt.

"Take this off," he commanded.

Immediately she pulled her shirt over her head and reached for the back clasp.

He stopped her hands before she could release the hooks.

"Wait."

Chapter Eleven

Bree stopped and dared not breathe. What? Did he have second thoughts? He didn't meet her eyes. Instead, his gaze was focused on her rather basic, more-function-than-fashion bra.

"You're so beautiful."

A gasp escaped her as he held his fingers just a hairsbreadth from her flesh. She could lean forward and force his touch, but that wasn't what she wanted. This was…mind-blowing, this worship, yet it was so heart-wrenchingly sincere. Her lips parted as she watched him, seeing her own chest rise and fall in anticipation as he barely grazed over the fullness of her breasts.

"Touch me, Bash." She couldn't help it, the words slipped from her. Just a whisper.

But he listened.

Still light as air, his fingers stroked the skin until it disappeared beneath the white lace. She closed her eyes and arched into his palms.

Her body quivered as his mouth replaced his fingers.

He kissed her through the material, yet she was conscious, barely conscious, of his fingers smoothing around her waist and up her back. How she didn't melt right there, she had no idea. Didn't care, either.

She could feel the roughness of the day's beard through the lacy satin. God, that was hot. Coupled with the moist heat of his mouth, it was damn near enough to push her over the edge.

The clasp fell loose, the weight of her breasts—so heavy and aching with the need for more attention—surprised her. As did the patience Bash had while tugging the straps down her arms, raising gooseflesh as his fingers slowly and gently brushed her skin.

"You're driving me nuts," she whispered. The laugh she tried to add ended up sounding like a whimper.

"You? I want to taste every inch of you, bit by bit. Honey, I don't think I'm going to make it."

"Me either."

She nearly came off his lap as his teeth closed around her swollen nipple. It wasn't that he hurt her, no. The light pressure-pain sent scorching quakes straight through her body until her pussy contracted with the need to be filled.

He cupped the other breast, rolling the nipple between his fingers as he alternated sucking and nibbling on the first. She clutched his hair, holding him there. Everything else faded. Or maybe they were transported to another place and time where there was nothing else, only her and Bash and this heady sensation that was only going to get more intoxicating.

"Now you," she said, forcing her throat to work. She tugged on his sleeve. "Take this off."

She helped him push it up over his head and then flung it carelessly behind her with a laugh. There was a recklessness in her blood, a confidence, some impulsive need to let go—really *let* go right now.

Nothing was going to stop her. If this was it, than it was going to be everything she'd every imagined and everything she could think of and—

Oh!

His mouth returned to her breast. He blew on the nipples, sending shivers throughout her body. Then he breathed hot on them, setting her on fire. Every sensation pooled between her thighs. She could reach down and release some of the tension, but that would not achieve what she wanted. For it to last forever.

Best she could, she memorized his flesh. Her fingers traced the creases on the muscles of his arms, tightly knotted cords beneath the skin that jumped as she touched them. That notched up her excitement—knowing she could affect him with such a simple gesture.

"Bed," she suggested. Her reach was limited and she wanted more—more access, more tasting, more heat. "C'mon."

Those large but gentle hands encircled her waist and practically lifted her off his lap. She whimpered at the loss of pressure against her clit, but knew soon it'd be replaced, even fulfilled, in a much better way.

She laughed.

"Get up there," he said, crawling on all fours the yard or so to the edge of the bed.

She complied, crawling up to the pillow.

"Nuh-uh. Come *here*." He patted the edge of the bed. "And lose those pants."

Her breath caught. His intentions were more than clear and it completely paralyzed her body with anticipation.

"Bree?" he teased.

Couldn't he see she was little more than a pile of mush? Still, she found the muscle coordination to reach for the zipper of her pants and loosen the button.

He reached the lower legs of the material and tugged. It both served to pull her over to him and slid her hips free. From there he quickly stripped them from her legs and tossed him into the dark abyss behind him. To the place where nothing mattered.

She really did like it here. Otherwise, she might feel a bit self-conscious that she was sitting on the bed with Bash between her knees.

"These are still in the way."

She gasped, clutched the comforter and nearly exploded at the intimate touch. God, who knew that such a light stroke right over the material that covered her swollen clit and pussy lips could be so...erotic. He probably could see how wet she got just from that slight touch.

"You like that?"

Before she could answer, he grabbed her thighs, pulled her closer to the edge of the bed and covered her with his hot mouth.

She clutched his hair, almost holding him away from short-circuiting her all at once with such an onslaught.

"Bash, no," she said when his mouth left her soaked panties and traveled down the inside of her thigh, alternating between tickling and nipping. The sudden flush that had hit her body was fading. Desperately she grabbed to hold on to it.

"I'll be back," he said, then traced a giant heart on her leg with his tongue. She shivered. "This is a dead end. I'll have to stop back here—" he touched her, shooting more sparks within her body. "Before exploring your other beautiful leg."

She moaned and leaned back, helpless to do anything, eager for him to hurry. But only so she could torture him the same way. And torture she would.

Thinking of devilish ways to pay him back for this was almost as arousing as what he did to her now.

His mouth was heaven and hell wrapped into one. A kiss on the underside of her knee, a bite on her inner thigh. She moaned and squirmed and tried to get him to come back to the middle—to the place that needed his attentions the most.

"Dammit, Bash," she gasped, almost laughing at the ticklish arcs of electricity that coursed through her bloodstream. "Get up here and kiss me proper."

"In a minute," he whispered.

Her body tensed against the new sensation of that hot air against her inner thigh. He was just starting the other leg, having teasingly bypassed her throbbing core.

"I'm busy."

Only Bash could say that and make it the sexiest thing in the world. Though, she doubted he could do anything at this moment to make the pounding need inside her go away. Except fill her.

She lay back on the bed and closed her eyes.

He must have been waiting for her surrender, because as soon as she did, his hot breath seared through her thin panties and caused her to jerk up, gasping. He pressed his mouth there, riding as she bucked against his persistent tongue.

The end was near. Or was it just the beginning? The muscles inside her quivered with the impending explosion. She ached to be filled with his thick, hard cock—and wanted to feel it throbbing inside her, pounding against her until he, too, found the release she craved.

"Bash!" she reached out and grasped his hair, holding his mouth there as she rocked her pussy against his face. There was no breathing, no heartbeat. Only the sensation of him against her swollen clit and flooding pussy. That's all she needed to live, right there, just this.

It hit her like a tidal wave. Blindsided her with the inability to think, breathe, speak, yet she heard her own moans and felt her body thrashing with the force of her orgasm.

And it kept going—Bash kept his tongue pressed to her clit. Even with the scrap of material between them, the constant back and forth motion seemed to extend the time her muscles spasmed. When she finally was able to form a coherent thought, her body felt limp with exhaustion.

Bash smiled and pressed a kiss to that secret spot that pushed her over the edge. He'd damn near came right along with her. Tasting her sweet come pouring through her panties and into his mouth, feeling her muscles bunch and jump beneath him was his undoing. This woman was more than he'd ever imagined. She had so much passion inside her, he felt like king of the world for having brought her to such a screaming pinnacle.

And he intended to do it again. And again.

But first, he was going to ask a favor of her. He didn't think there'd need to be any begging.

He pressed his lips to her soft belly, reveling in the way her muscles reacted by shuddering just beneath the skin. So responsive. So eager. He was so fucking hard he wasn't going to last much longer.

"You're so beautiful. And you smell so good. I could eat you up."

He could too. He'd never be tired of lapping up her juices and sucking that sweet bud of her clit.

"Hmmm," she sighed, her chest humming under his lips as he made his way up her body. Despite the burning desperation in his loins, he paused at her luscious breasts. Neither too big nor too small. He cupped them in his hands, suckling one then the other nipple, marveling at the way the peaks tightened beneath his tongue.

Her breath hitched. He loved the way she reacted. God, was he going to miss this. He'd think about it every day. Imagine this very moment, with his body nearly covering hers, the taste of her come in his mouth, the warm silk of her skin against his rough palms.

This was heaven. There was nowhere else for him to go from here.

"Scoot up," he said, dropping a kiss just over her precious heart. Amazing how he could feel it beating so close to the skin there. The way he felt shocked him—half of him wanted to pull her so close and wrap her into his arms forever. The other half was eager to fuck her until there really was nothing else. He wanted to shatter the ceiling of the universe tonight.

Hell, maybe he could do both.

He rolled to the side as she pulled her legs up onto the bed. Quickly dispatching the rest of his clothes, he watched her. His mouth watered looking at her. It was like a dream come true to have her here. Again. He climbed up against her and stretched against her curves. There'd never be enough touching her.

Finding her lips, he nudged them open and explored her mouth again. His muscles bunched she moaned against him, licking her own flavor from his mouth with such relish. That's what he wanted, to have her mouth feasting up on him with such fervor.

He kneaded her breast and rocked against her sex. "I want something," he said between kisses. Her nails raked over his shoulders. Control nearly disappeared when she hiked a leg over his and rubbed her soaking wet pussy against his cock. What he wouldn't give to sheathe himself inside her in one fulfilling momentum.

Not yet.

"I want you to suck me."

He smiled against her mouth as her tongue darted into his mouth wrapped around his. Her hands were suddenly all over him, touching, squeezing, rubbing his flesh, exploring crevices and generally forcing all rational thought from him. Just when he thought she couldn't get sexier.

She made her way down his body. When she paused to flick her tongue over his flat nipples, he had to grip the base of his cock to keep from letting go. Damn, he'd always had control. He had to work up a come, not work at holding back until he was ready.

Bree did this to him. Only she could. Those hands. Her hands, roaming over him like embers burning his flesh. But such sweet pain.

Her mouth was worse. Had it been like this for her? God, he hoped so. He wanted her to know such mind-numbing sensations.

He yelped when her fingers slid down the length of his cock and then encircled him tightly, drawing up. He forced himself to think of something. Anything else. But her scent — the scent on his own lips from feasting on her sweetness — wafted up to tease him.

"Bree, I-I — "

"Shut up." She placed a hand on his chest and pushed him back onto the bed.

He moaned, but didn't fight. As if he could. A woman with her hand sliding up and over his cock with the damn near perfect combination of motion and pressure — well, she had control of the situation.

"My turn."

Instead of gracing him with her hot, wet mouth taking him in, she instead bent to bite the sensitive flesh of his inner thigh. "Oh God."

"Told you it was my turn."

The confident lilt in her voice sealed his fate.

While her hand kept his cock at the center of attention, her mouth teased all around. He lifted his hips, begging for her. He even opened his eyes when she used her fingers to sweep the pearl of come from the tip of his cock and suck her fingers.

"Christ, Bree." Sweat poured from his body. His muscles shook with the tension that coursed through them.

Yet he was fixated with the way her lovely lips pursed and parted as she once again tasted him...without touching him.

Then she tucked her hair over to one side and leaned over. He couldn't see. That just made it worse, knowing her mouth was so close. He arched up, trying to find her seeking mouth. How he wanted to hold her head there and pump between those lips until he blew his entire load down her throat, then watch her creamy neck as she swallowed it.

He groaned and fisted her hair, pushing her head down to him.

That groan turned into a wild growl as she simply lapped the pre-come from the head of his cock.

"Think you've had enough torture?"

Little consolation that her breath hitched a bit when she spoke. He knew she was all aroused again. Could smell it lingering in the room. "Bree..."

"Damn!" he shouted as her mouth closed over his cock and sucked. Hard.

One hand cupped his balls, the other pumped up and down, twisting as she did in some myriad of motion that removed any ability to rationalize what she was doing. Higher and higher she took him. How he hadn't simply burst like a dam in her mouth, he didn't know.

When his cock head hit the back of her throat and slid against it, those lips closing over the base of his shaft, he moaned and clamped his teeth together. Toe-curling. Never understood that phrase before now.

"Jesus Christ, woman!" With a moan, he fisted her hair, careful not to hurt her, and stroked his cock and in out of her. The sound of her sucking and lapping did him in.

"Take it," he commanded, forgetting to breathe, forgetting everything but the velvety recesses of her hot moist cavern as he pumped. "It's yours."

She sucked. Christ, how did she do that to him? Instead of waiting for the force of his come to propel his seed, she pulled it from him. He grasped anything he could to hold on to reality.

Didn't matter.

She drove him over the edge with that fast-moving tongue and velvety hands. He was barely aware of her name falling from his lips as he came, draining the essence of him into her beautiful mouth.

Chapter Twelve

Bash closed his eyes and wrapped his arms around Bree. She'd crawled back up and lay beside him, her head on his shoulder.

He wasn't done with her, but this intimate moment where they paused to catch their breath—it reaffirmed the knowledge that they had something special. This wasn't a matter of scratching an itch or giving into lust. They should have been together all along.

Bree's fingers traced over his chest. Cold chills raced through his body. He loved her. Not that he hadn't known it before, but dammit, he *loved* her. Enough to give up everything else. Never had his heart felt so full, so complete.

What a damn mirage that was.

"What's wrong?"

"Nothing, love. Just trying to get up enough strength to do this." He nuzzled her neck until she laughed and rolled over.

Then he groaned and climbed over her, straddling her hips and looking down into those liquid eyes.

His cock was more than ready to start round two. He lifted his hips and positioned it at her slick entrance, watching her face as he nudged between her swollen lips.

She wriggled against him, pushing him into her. Her mouth was parted, and she panted her plea for him to fill her up.

Not willing to disappoint her, even for the sake of teasing, he pushed into her tightness, moaning as her pussy walls gripped and pulled him in. He had to pause there, his body fully encased inside hers, and gathered his bearings. Their heartbeats were tangible, throbbing against one another.

He held her gaze while sliding out just an inch before pushing back in. Her head fell back, her mouth open in a silent gasp. He heard her. Deep in his soul he heard her plea.

Faster and faster, harder and harder he pumped, each time a little deeper, a little more intense. Both of their bodies were slick with sweat. Her hair fanned out on the pillow, her cheeks pink, eyes glossy as she searched for the peak. *I'll show you the way*, he promised silently, committing to memory the rapturous look on her face.

Her fingers tightened around his biceps, her hips lifting and grinding against his frenzied thrusts, pushing, driving.

"Bree!"

The world shattered. Light spiked, electricity coursed through his body as her pussy walls milked him with their viselike clamp. She joined him, fingers cutting into his flesh as she screamed and bucked under him. Her come rushed over him, sending aftershocks through his body.

He closed his eyes against the unspeakable level of pleasure he felt, praying he could conserve even one ounce of this feeling.

Bree lifted her hands and cupped his face.

Tears sprung to his eyes. Squeezing them shut, he pushed through her hands and buried his face against her neck. There he inhaled her scent and waited for the wave of pure agony to pass over him.

"Bash?"

Praying his eyes were clear, he let her push him off of her and smiled wryly. "Sorry, babe. I just can't get enough of you."

"Something's wrong."

He took her hand, such a small, pale hand in his grease-stained, scar-littered grasp. "Bree, I—"

"Bash, wait. Shh." She pulled her hand free and pushed it against his lips.

He paused, concentrating watching her and listening. His gut twisted, fearing what he knew had to be inevitable.

Luke.

If he'd approached him outside, there's no reason he couldn't walk into this very room and destroy them.

He waited, like a man faced with the gallows. Waited for him to appear and Bree to wrench from his embrace to tearfully apologize to the man she'd lost two years ago.

"Never mind," she said, shaking her head. "I just…"

"What?" He dreaded this, but it had to happen.

"It felt like…like someone was here. Watching us."

He pushed away and stood up, immediately missing the heat of her body, but flipped on the brighter, overhead light. It was more of an act than the truth, but he looked around. "No one's here, Brehann. You locked the back door, right? There's no way anyone could get in."

She sat up and pulled covers up to her chest. He still saw it heaving in what he could only guess was anticipation, perhaps fear. "No, but…"

But. Funny how that word was as sharp as a fucking sword right now. "We need to talk. There are some...things you need to know."

"Shh!" she commanded.

He froze, feeling much too vulnerable standing there naked between the bed and light switch.

A flicker of movement near the bathroom door caught his eye. He whirled, swearing he saw Luke's face. Winking.

Winking?

What the hell did that mean? It was time to learn exactly what that was all about. He strode off toward that doorway.

Empty.

"Stop playing with me," he warned, praying his whisper didn't carry. "What are you doing?"

Silence.

"Bash?" Bree called.

"Just a second, hon."

He ran the cold water and splashed it on his face, using the mirror to watch behind him. There was no telling what power Luke had in his ghostly state, or what his intentions could be.

"Stay away from her." He just hoped his warning was heeded.

Luke had no idea what he'd be willing to do to make sure Bree was safe.

"Bash!"

Her scream tore him from the sink and to her. She was still sitting on the bed, covers now pulled up to her chin. Her eyes darted from him to the wall.

"What? What is it?" Bash sat down beside her and pulled her against his shoulder.

"He's here."

So low, so…afraid and even innocent. Fear. That's what dampened her voice and caused her body to shake. Was he sure? Or was it laced with guilt, smothered with regret?

"How do you know?"

"The light." She pointed. On the computer table, a small light glowed. "Only he'd do that. But why? What is he doing here?"

He squinted, then got up to look. She tried to pull him back, but he had to see. Had to know. It was a novelty light, a neon Chevrolet sign no bigger than his hand. Nightlight, likely.

Only it wasn't plugged in.

* * * * *

"Throw it away," Bree commanded.

Bash tilted his head. "You sure?"

"Positive. Time I did anyway. That was his, not mine. Kept meaning to give it away or something. But now— now I don't care. He's gone, Bash. Gone. Out of my life."

"What about all the things you've held on to for two years?" He found it hard that she could flip a switch so quickly and easily.

"I've got something else to hold on to. You were the one I've dreamed and fantasized about, Bash. He's gone. You're helping me to let go."

He kissed her forehead and prayed she really could let go. The thought of Luke still had her reacting. He didn't like that one bit. "It's been a long day, sweetheart. I think we're both strung way too tight and imagining things. You go to sleep. I'm here. I'm staying right here and holding you all night long."

"You sure?"

Bash relaxed, hearing the sleepiness in her voice. "I'm sure."

He reached up and tugged the switch for the overhead light, extinguishing it. Then he turned off the bedside lamp, plunging them into darkness.

He lay beside Bree, listening to her even breaths as she slept. At least one of them could. The door was tightly closed, the windows locked. He hated to have the overhead fan on, the humming noise blocking out what would be the first hint someone was in the room with him, but it was too damn stuffy not to have some form of circulation.

The ghostly light that had turned Bree from a hot, passionate woman into a frightened, nervous girl had faded just moments after he'd picked it up. Despite her words, Bash sensed doubt in her voice. He wanted to think that she was saying things she'd only thought, making statements she was almost afraid to feel. Letting go of the security of the pain.

But she knew.

Luke was here.

God, what was he going to do? He rubbed his forehead and wished he could see Bree. Just watch her sleep. Had Luke done that? Had he ever truly cherished her the way she deserved.

You know I didn't, came the words.

The sound seemed to swirl on the breeze created by the whirring ceiling fan. Had he imagined that?

This was new. A mind-reading ghost. He rolled over and hugged Bree to his chest. *Mine.*

Don't blow it, buddy.

"Blow it? What?"

"Bash?" Bree's sleepy voice drifted back.

He snuggled her closer. "Hmmm?"

"Who're you talking to?" He could barely understand her muffled words.

A dream or did she hear Luke, too? "No one. Shh."

He sighed and pretended to be sleeping, but he knew there'd be precious little of that tonight.

He was wrong. When he opened his eyes again, the faint morning light painted the room gray. As he blinked, the silhouettes of the furniture became more defined. So did the figure standing at the foot of the bed.

All his muscles tightened. Somehow he kept from jumping up, probably that tiny shred of common sense functioning at this hour that didn't want Bree to witness this.

"Why are you here?" he hissed, slowly untangling his arm from around Bree. When she moaned, they both fell silent.

"You shouldn't have come back."

"Why? Why?" And why was he having this conversation *with a ghost*? Had he been wrong all this time—was Luke tied into the car? Or maybe he'd been here with Bree the whole time, watching over her.

But if that were the case, how had someone been able to get in and destroy? "You set me up. You did it, didn't you?"

"Bash?"

Groan. "Shh. Go back to sleep."

She pulled away and sat up. "I heard you. Who were you talking to?"

He wasn't going to able to keep denying things. The shadow at the end of the bed disappeared, but that mattered little. He was still here.

Bash would have to come clean with her soon, very soon. In the meantime… "Huh? Musta been dreaming. What'd I say?"

She relaxed, but not completely. "There's something… Wait."

Her entire body went rigid.

If only he could see what she saw or hear what she heard. Straining, his senses picked up nothing. Could Luke be talking to her?

"He's here, isn't he? It wasn't a dream last night. The light and all."

Bash rolled over and tried to hug Bree.

"Hold on." She didn't push him away, but simply stopped him from tossing his arm over her. She was silent for a few moments, only their breathing audible. "You're going to think I'm nuts."

This had to be a dream. This was the furthest from predictable he could have imagined. Unless he was all wrong. Somehow, that would be even more farfetched. "Of course I won't."

Bash propped himself up against the headboard and pulled her close to him. This time she complied, even laying her head on his chest. "Are you getting the same feeling I am that we've woken up in some..."

To that she laughed. Such a beautiful sound to wake up to. "Some..."

"Strange dimension? Dream world?" Spurred on by her playfulness, he tried to come up with another description for this wonderful feeling of waking up beside the woman he loved.

She nodded, the smile on her face brighter than any sun. "That sounds about right."

"But—" he started.

"Shh. Wait." She sat up and leaned forward.

The light was stronger now, the sun reaching in around the blinds and illuminating the room enough to show her features. Her eyes were closed, her held tilted almost as if she were listening for something. Or to someone.

The corner of her mouth twitched, as if almost smiling.

"Did you hear that?" she asked, turning her eyes to him. They glistened with excitement, her smile now brighter than the morning sun.

It was hard not to smile, even though his chest felt so painfully tight in dread of what she was going to say. He shook his head. "Tell me."

"Bash, I think Luke's here. I thought I'd be afraid if this ever happened. Thought I'd be smothered with guilt. But I'm not." She rattled at the speed of sound, her voice half an octave higher than normal.

Naturally. *Twist the knife, Luke, go on.* Since his best friend hadn't been able to keep them apart while he was alive, he was trying everything he could to keep them apart after his death. That's why Luke had come to him outside, to warn him off. He was setting him up by destroying his clothes, trying to paint Bash as jealous and vengeful. Now he was going to Bree, probably feeding her some bullshit story about him. "Luke? Honey, he's dead. Are you telling me you've seen Luke's ghost?"

"Seen? No." She shook her head and grabbed his hands and shaking them—bouncing the whole bed with her. "Oh my God, Bash, I *heard* him. He spoke to me. He apologized for all the wrong things he did while he was alive and said he was sorry for making me feel so guilty when it was all his fault."

She reached out and touched his face. "I can't believe it. I mean. He's here, Bash. Can't you hear him? Of course, my God, a ghost. Isn't that incredible? He said there was so much he wanted to tell me, but he doesn't have much time."

"I'm sure he said something about me being here, then didn't he?"

Her face fell. A-ha. He knew it.

"He warned me to guard my heart." The tilt of her eyebrow was almost challenging. As if daring him. Sure, she had Luke there to back her up. Had he said he'd kick his ass if he hurt her too?

Bash clenched his teeth. That wasn't something Luke would say. Obviously he'd learned a thing or two about what to say to women. Or he was being coached. To that he nearly laughed. Maybe *he* was nuts. "That's not wrong advice, Bree. Were the roles reversed, I'd probably tell you to make sure you looked at all choices before making a decision. Just remember," he said as he slipped out of her bed. "I'm here. He's not. And I do love you."

For how long? He couldn't answer that. But suddenly things just got a lot more complicated. Not only was the Corvette here for him, but Luke was working an angle to take Bree away from him. What were the chances he could escape both and come out the victor?

He walked into the bathroom and splashed cold water on his face. Not that he needed it to wake up him, but rather, to tamper the insecurity and doubt he felt. Everything had been perfect before this big spectral appearance. What the hell?

As he looked in the mirror, he spotted Luke standing behind him, arms crossed, devilish smile on his face.

* * * * *

Bree stared at Bash over their quickie breakfast of toaster waffles and orange juice. What an enigma.

She'd expected him to talk her out of believing in ghosts. At least laugh and say that was one hell of a vivid dream. Only, it hadn't been a dream. She'd been wide awake. It could only mean one thing. Bash knew Luke was here. In fact, now that she thought about it, it probably explained those times she'd caught Bash literally talking to himself.

To Luke, that is.

"You knew, didn't you?" she asked before she second-guessed her logic.

"Knew what?"

She took a gulp of juice while watching his fork slide from between his lips. Lips that had nuzzled her neck while she'd poured their glasses, his hands sliding around her belly and hugging her. She could so get used to having him here in the morning. However, she wondered just how he felt to share the house with a ghost.

She put her glass down and waited until he met her eyes. "You knew Luke was here."

He cut another piece of waffle and then answered. "When I went outside. Before you…"

"Yeah, yeah. I'm sorry about that." Her eyes flitted to the red and purple bump on his forehead.

He rolled his eyes. "The facts here. I went outside to check on the garage door. I heard someone talking. Luke. He said something about destiny having its own plan and not changing it." He waved his hand and speared the last bit of waffle with his fork, then used it to sop up some of the syrup. "Then he was gone. But the car was there. I heard you scream, I came inside. I got walloped. End of story." He shrugged and popped the forkful into this mouth. "I think he was responsible for that light too."

"Probably right. Why didn't you say anything?" She didn't understand why he'd keep it a secret.

She ignored the deadpan look.

"Please," he chuckled. "You would have thought me insane, probably insisted there was some ulterior motive for even bringing it up, and well, last thing I want was for you to doubt how I feel about you. We went through enough yesterday."

He was right. Dead on with that one. She would have laughed at him if he'd have suggested such a thing. "So now what? Last night I got the impression you'd be leaving soon. You're not, are you?"

"Hell, no."

Good. She smiled up at him, loving the way his mouth twisted into a grin, one side lifting a bit higher than the other. But there were questions in his eyes. "I don't want you to leave."

The shadows cleared and his smile opened wider. "Glad we've cleared that up. Can I stay in your room, too?"

"I demand it." She couldn't stop grinning. Could her heart withstand sitting here every morning with him? It felt like it'd burst now, just thinking about it. Not that they'd discussed the future beyond the next, what? Week? But a replay of the night before clouded her thoughts. There had been hints of goodbye in their kisses. She had to know. "How long will you be here?"

He blinked. Shock. He hadn't expected her to be so abrupt.

"I-I don't know."

She stared at her plate. So much for getting her hopes up. How did Luke showing up tie into all this? Or did it? No. She swallowed. That was trying to read too much into things. He'd had positive things to say about Bash. If her brain wasn't so foggy about his exact words, she'd swear he was encouraging their relationship—albeit with caution. Oh, it was so confusing! Speculation did little to answer the questions that formed during each of these conversations. She cleared her throat and forced the word past her tight throat. "Why?"

"I mean—"

She looked back up and watched him push his hand through his sleep-tousled hair.

"Okay. How about this— I will not leave on my own accord." He said it slowly, as if testing those words.

Sounded like a riddle. She didn't like games, not when it came to this. But it certainly was a better answer than "I don't know".

"Okay," she responded, picking up her plate and reaching for his. "You're welcome here as long as you can stay."

"Good." He grabbed her arm as she reached for his glass. "Because I want to stay forever. But destiny has a funny way of changing our plans."

Bree should have felt euphoric. After all, hadn't her dream come true? Bash was here, pledged to stay on, had admitted he loved her and continued to shower her with attention.

And it wasn't Luke. She'd been so afraid when she'd heard that voice. Despite all the clues, the hints, the nagging in the back of her mind, she'd fought believing in ghosts, especially in Luke's ghost, until he'd addressed her directly. There had been no denying that voice and the way he'd spoken her name.

But her initial twinge of fear and guilt had faded, as if he controlled some sort of magic. She hadn't told Bash everything he'd said. Like that he wanted her to be happy with Bash, that now he could see his errors and was sorry for them, and was glad she'd turned to Bash and not a stranger that wouldn't cherish her the way she deserved.

She rubbed her eyes, feeling the overflow of emotions leaking out her tear ducts. *Dammit, Luke!* She smiled to herself.

"Bree?"

She turned off the water and dried her hand on the towel before turning to Bash, who stood just inside the back door. "Yeah?" Damn, he looked good. Snug jeans, gray T-shirt that already had a few smudges of dirt. He'd been out getting started on her car. "That was fast. Done already?" She doubted he'd time to do more than open the garage door and turn on the lights.

"There's something you should see."

Not good. He wasn't smiling.

"What?" Dozens of scenarios ran through her head, from their cars being trashed to another Luke appearance to... "I'm coming."

She reached for his hand and walked beside him.

The garage looked fine. At least it hadn't collapse or caught on fire or...not that she could have slept through something like that.

"All I did was open it up. I didn't do this. I hope you trust me."

The muscle there at the edge of his jaw twitched and his eyes were hard as steel. Why was he saying that? Why would she accuse him?

He nudged the door, swinging it open.

She gasped and stepped forward. The rest of the posters had been ripped from the wall and sprinkled over everything like confetti.

"Oh my God." It wasn't the posters or the turned over toolbox that concerned her. Or even her car. But Bash's. "Your car!"

She rushed to it and started swiping at the paper that would hide any damage. Bash appeared beside her and pulled her arm away. "The cars are fine. But look around. It's all trashed. Everything." He led her to the vise that had been wrenched from the metal worktable and then pointed to the air compressor. The hose was shredded.

She didn't understand. Bash hadn't done this. He wouldn't. Couldn't. There hadn't been enough time and...she looked again at the toppled five-foot toolbox. Could he have done it alone?

Could a ghost do it?

Why? "Why?" she said again, out loud. Seemed to be about the only thing coming out of her mouth these days. "Did Luke do this?"

Bash had let go of her and was starting to pick up the tools that were littered everywhere. How everything had fallen and not so much as scratched either vehicle was just too...eerie.

"Yes. Luke did this." Bash's voice was flat, his eyes dark. She didn't like the defeat in the slump of his shoulders. "He thinks he's helping you by erasing all signs of him in your life. He trashed the closet, too, if I guess correctly. I don't understand his motivations, but they're not sinister. At least toward you. I don't think he wants me around."

"He does." Bree snatched the ratchet out of his hand. "He told me. He's glad I'm with you and not someone else. But there were warnings attached to that. He's afraid you'll hurt me."

Bash's brow creased as he surveyed the garage again. "I don't get it."

"Tell me about the car." Women's intuition or simply sensitivity to the subject, but she knew this would present one of the biggest hurdles she could imagine.

"No. Not yet."

"Yes. I need to know, dammit. If you're staying here, living with me and this...ghost." She closed her eyes and laughed. Oh, how ridiculous this all sounded. What would her friends even *think* if she suggested such a thing, yet here they were acting as if it were nothing. *Yeah, just move in with me and the ghost of my fiancé. He likes you.*

"You don't want to hear about it right now."

"Probably not. But I need to. We've covered Luke's part in this. So who's in the car?"

"Technically, no one."

"Oh God. What's that mean?" Was he playing with her? "Another ghost."

"Come here." She took his hand and let him lead her to the front seat of his car, then got in beside her. Then he rewound their fingers together. "This isn't going to be easy to tell you. I thought it'd get easier, that there'd be an opportune time to tell you this. But there hasn't been."

She was so cold. So afraid. What he said was going to sever everything they'd forged together. Erase all their promises. It was there, in his eyes.

He released her fingers and pushed his hair off his forehead before turning back to her. "That car, Bree, is here for me. Only thing I can figure is that it's been taunting you to get to me, to pin me down. It has no reason to come after you."

"Bash—"

"Let me talk. Let me spit this out, once and for all."

His fingers turned white where he gripped the steering wheel. He stared at the gauges while his chest rose and fell with jagged breaths. She understood that, her own chest felt constricted.

"From the beginning. The night…" He turned to her and gathered both her hands. "The night that Luke died. He came to my house and confronted me. I defended you, swore I loved you and vowed never to hurt you, but of course, you know Luke, he was full of rage. And going to kill you. I really feared he'd do it."

She shook her head. No. No. Luke had never made it to Bash's house. That was the story she'd gotten. "But…"

"Listen. Trust me love, I could keep this secret forever and continue on like we were, but you don't deserve that. And I can't keep it in. The guilt is eating me up. The car is closing in and now Luke is here, for God only knows what reason. Listen."

She felt his tension through to his tightening fingers. But he didn't hurt her. He had control there, and took a few deep breaths before continuing.

"I got in the car with Luke and we came back here to try to catch you before you left. We were going to talk it out, all of us. But you were already gone. I'm glad you were. He needed to know that you were strong enough. I was proud of you, even though I knew it was just postponing another confrontation."

"It was on the way back to my house that the accident happened—"

Chapter Thirteen

"No! No!" she gasped. "It can't be." He was suggesting...

"I can't even remember what happened, Bree. The car swerved. Maybe a tire blew. Maybe Luke just lost it."

"But..." It wasn't true. None of it. Couldn't be. Yet Bash painted a picture with his words that she could see clearly, as if a movie were playing out there on the windshield of the car.

"The whole car caught on fire. I pulled Luke out. He made me promise to look after you."

His voice cracked, then trailed off and he looked out over the length of the hood. He spoke the truth.

She couldn't stand it. Tears poured from her eyes. How could he have faced that? It tore into her just to hear him say it. No wonder he'd stayed gone for two years. The horror must have been...

"Then the ambulance came and took us both to the hospital. I fought so hard. I wanted to stay here. I knew Luke was gone. He'd died right there in my arms, with your name his last breath."

She reached out, desperate to comfort the ache she saw there, *felt* herself. But he would have none of that. It seemed like he had wrapped himself in his own agony. Was almost numb.

He continued, his voice losing emotion, becoming a monotone. "It was so dark, but only for a second. I knew what had happened. My injuries were as bad as Luke's. Fighting was no use."

She sat there frozen, unable to move, unable to think. What was he saying? How could this be? Tears fell silently from her eyes as she watched him. He didn't look at her at all now, simply clutched one of her hands and wrapped the other around the steering wheel.

"It's like they say, those people who come back. You see your body lying there, like looking down on it while the doctors pump at your chest and shoot the body full of adrenaline. Then there's a white light. I watched Luke go into it. He reached back, already apologetic."

"But I fought. I turned away from the light and ran. It was like swimming against the current, but all I could think about was you. About how you were going to feel when you came back from your weekend of fun and learned we were both dead. How neither of us got to explain. How Luke had asked me — pleaded with me to take care of you. I couldn't give up."

"I roamed the darkness for days, then weeks, months, years. It was some strange place between life and death that wasn't heaven and wasn't hell. I don't know how else to explain it. It's nothing you can imagine. I had no body, there was nothing there — just emptiness. It was almost worse than having gone on to the place I was supposed to go — the sense of loss, emptiness, failure. Guilt. It was all I knew."

The words hung heavy in the interior of the car. This had to be shock, this feeling of disbelief and amazement. Yet it cut so jagged in her chest. She felt every heartbeat as it pounded, and every breath was filled with razor-sharp needles. Still, it had to be nothing compared to what he described. She couldn't fathom such loss, such emptiness.

But there it was, written on his face like a fresh, open wound.

Bash had died in the crash.

No. He hadn't. Couldn't have. But she knew damn well he could have. She had been in a daze for weeks, numb and in shock that it had been possible. Bash had been in that hospital, alone. Suffering, dealing with it all and then losing the battle.

Her breath hitched. There was no stopping the dam of tears that flowed freely down her cheeks. Bash was dead. And she never knew it.

Yet that didn't explain that she held his hand right now, flesh and bone. That he looked exactly the same as he had before she'd left—not burnt and battered from the crash that had torn Luke's body apart. He was right though. She couldn't have, wouldn't have even thought about accepting this story as truth before today. Still, the war of pain and sadness and determination that lined Bash's face and milked tears from his eyes forced her to consider. What if he *was* telling the truth? "I-I-I didn't know…"

"I figured that out. I can't answer to how it happened that no one told you. Perhaps to spare you? According to the records—and there was only a tiny obituary—my parents had my body shipped up to the family cemetery in Tennessee, cremated and the ashes buried between my grandparents."

This was a new flash of guilt. She would have gone. Would have sent flowers, anything. Something. She would have cried for him. Failure to do that seemed like an enormous weight. "No, Bash, they did tell me. Everyone came up and tried to console me, hugged me and said it was so terrible to lose both of you. I simply thought that they'd known you'd run away. Left town, whatever explanation I had been given. It makes sense. Oh God. Why didn't I know? How could I have not understood it when they said both you and Luke were gone?"

He reached out then, placing that warm, vibrant hand over her heart. "It's because you knew, here, that I wasn't really gone. I've been here. I fought and searched and roamed in the darkness, following my heart blindly. I had to get back to you. Thoughts of you kept me going, kept me searching. I knew what we'd had was real and I'd have given anything in those dark days just to hear you say my name, to feel your touch. Imagining that I'd have these last few days with you…it's like a dream come true."

She sobbed and held his hand there, over her heart, promising with each beat that she'd never, ever love anyone else, pledging herself to him—no matter what. Even if this were true, if it all ended right now, she'd love him forever.

"I've got to finish. The car—the '67 Chevy Corvette— that's all that's left of the darkness that threatened to swallow me up. It will follow me for the rest of my time here, waiting to take me back to the place I belong. Consider it the grim reaper of the lost souls. Only I'm not lost, Bree. As long as I'm with you, I'm not lost."

It was too much. What happened to normal life? What happened to boy meets girl, boy and girl fall in love, get married, have kids, live happily every after? Bash was, essentially, saying he was…

"I was finally able to cross back into this world on the anniversary of my death. It was as if I'd never left. There I was, in this car, pulling out of the railroad parking lot and heading straight for your house the way I'd dreamed of doing, over and over. Two years I'd waited to see you again. And it was so worth it. Even if all I have is this last week with you, Brehann, it was so worth two years of searching."

She tried to breathe, but it was so tight, so hard to understand, to comprehend.

"Please. This sounds like I came back just to disrupt your life and cause you heartache all over again. I never wanted that. Would have stayed away if I'd have known I'd do that to you. I-I..." He slapped the steering wheel and rubbed his cheek. "I expected I'd get to see you from afar. When my car broke down I never expected you to still be here, much less still recognize me. Do you know how...*alive* I felt when I knew you had cherished and remembered what we'd had together? But then things got away, and I knew, every day I stayed, every time I came over, it was going to make it harder not to hurt you."

So many questions. "Why doesn't anyone else recognize you?" Her mother had gasped in horror, but referred to him as looking like Bash. The guy at the parts shop. How many others?

"I don't know. Maybe because they know it can't be me. I don't know how I even have this body when the newspaper said I was cremated. Luke's a true ghost. He's been to the other side and is here on a mission—but he can't take human form. I never crossed that line, never walked into the light. I don't have any special powers, not like Luke. And trust me, his appearance here is a mystery to me."

"I-I don't know what to say. I mean, my mind is screaming this is one helluva science fiction story, but my heart feels. Oh, God, my chest hurts. My heart aches. How-how can this be?"

"You can't understand. It's like the laws of religion and math and gravity and all those things you learned in school." He laughed then. "You just have to accept. It's me, Sebastian Bernecchi. I'm technically just a lost soul."

"What does this mean for us?" she asked after a good fifteen minutes of silence had passed.

"It means I love you too much to stay, to put you through the horror of living like this. I can't support you. We can't get married. And we'll have a damn black Corvette breathing down our — my — neck at every turn."

She hadn't entirely digested this whole thing. Hell, when it finally sunk in, she'd probably commit herself to the asylum, but when it came down to it, she had Bash. Here. Right this minute, professing to love her. He said he wasn't actually alive, but he was flesh and blood. She could feel his pulse in his wrist, had heard his heartbeat against his chest. There wasn't much more alive than that.

"Listen, sweetheart. I promised you I'd stay here as long as I could. Why don't we get the car fixed and then we'll go spend the rest of the day together?" He pressed a kiss to her forehead. "This wasn't how I wanted to tell you. I blurted it all out and you probably don't believe half of it. I'm sorry. So sorry. But I had to tell you before something happened."

"Like what?"

"You could have heard from any number of people that I was dead. I didn't want you or anyone else to think I was some imposter taking advantage."

"I know —"

"I know. But the car's out there, just waiting for me. To take me back. And there won't be another chance."

Surreal. Any minute now she'd wake up and they'd laugh over such a ridiculous notion. But the way Bash squeezed her fingers was all too real. Long minutes passed while she tried to digest this. She could only guess what was going through his mind.

"Come on," he finally said. "Let's get this done."

"What about this mess?" She pointed out the window.

"We'll clean up. I bet Luke left what we needed to fix your car. He's looking out for you."

"I know," she said. Luke had come to release her. To free her from the bonds he held after all this time. To cast his blessing. That meant so much to her. Left her free to love Bash with everything she had.

She got out of the car and stood in the garage. Despite their conversation, these bizarre revelations had lifted that feeling of guilt that had anchored her to the past. While Bash certainly had professed to a miserable two years, she essentially had a giant void in her life. No more.

Regardless of what happened.

"Well, let's not waste any more time. Not if you're saying we don't have very much left."

She nearly melted at the sight of his sad, crooked smile.

Bree refused to dwell on his words, but somehow she found herself stopping from their work of cleaning the garage to look at him. *Ghost?* Mind-boggling. How can one have sex with a ghost? He bruised and bled—she'd hit him on the head and he'd bled, for chrissake.

But then he'd smile at her like he knew what she was thinking, sometimes even wink. And she realized it didn't matter.

The feeling inside her was real enough.

"Okay." He rubbed his hands down his pants and left dark streaks in their wake. She tried to use a red shop rag to clean up, to little avail. Her hands were stained.

"The hose for the air compressor is shot. We need a new one of those. The pump should be in, too. Here."

Bash handed her a wad of bills. This should more than cover it.

"Whoa. Where'd this come from? Ghosts can't have money." She didn't know that, but he'd said he couldn't support her.

He winked. "No, but I do remember where Luke had stashed his garage money. He's not going to use it and I would think he'd want to make sure you have a dependable ride."

"Right." She unfolded the money and gasped at the number of large bills. "This was in here. All this time?" If she only would have looked, have cleaned out the way Luke had come back from the grave to do. When it was done, it would be her garage. She wouldn't feel guilty to stack flowerpots on the shop bench and prop up her rake near the door.

"So, we're going to get this?"

"You are."

There were two cars, one of which was not fit to drive a block, much less the distance to the parts shop. The other was not hers and she wasn't going to even try it. "I'll go with you. Come on."

"I trust you, babe. Here." He tossed her the keys. She swallowed and stared at them, lying there in her palm. If his story were true, how'd he come by a car like this anyway?

"I can't." She tried to hand the keys back.

"I've nearly got this off by hand already. I can have it all ready for new part by the time you get back. I want this done so I know you'll be safe on the road. But I don't want to waste all day working on it."

He wasn't going. Losing battle. She knew it. Had seen that look before.

"I want to go down on record stating that I think this is a really bad idea."

"You don't want to spend the day with me? Outside of the garage, that is?"

"You know better."

"You'll be fine." Bash wrapped his arms around her waist and kissed her nose. "Things are different around here. It's your car, too. Now go on."

Her car? "Wait. Mine?" She squinted at the blue Chevy, wondering when she'd missed that revelation.

He shrugged. "Blue as your eyes. All I can think was that you were the vehicle that brought me back here. It translated into that. I know I lied about it from the beginning. I shouldn't have, but what else could I have said? But it's yours as much as mine."

She didn't know what she was going to say, but it was barely a croak that made it past her throat.

Comprehension was blurred by the feel of his mouth against hers, his gentle tongue brushing over her lower lip, then nudging them open and pushing his way inside.

She moaned and clutched his shirt, tilting her head to allow him the deepest access possible. So much passion. So much feeling in just the simple gesture. But the same, the desperation level ratcheted up a notch when she stroked her tongue over his. She felt his erection pressing against her lower belly. Her own sex was on fire, even her body's natural fluids worked to fan the flames rather than extinguish them.

"Go," he said, rocking against her. "Go so we can get this car done and get around to some of that."

She needed no more prodding.

"Shit." She couldn't even reach the pedals.

"On the side. Pull the lever."

She did and the bench seat slid forward a couple of notches. Much better.

The clutch was a killer. While Bash hit the electric garage opener, she tested the gearshift out and then started the car.

It purred to life, like a little kitten. She knew though, unleashed it was like a hungry tiger. Hopefully she could keep a handle on it.

"I don't know about this," she reiterated to Bash through the open window. "I can't get a feel for this clutch and gas pedal."

What she got in return was a blown kiss and a thumbs-up.

Gee, thanks. "Love you," she mouthed back.

She killed it backing up. Expecting him to come storming out, stony-faced, she hurriedly restarted it and pulled out of the driveway. After damn near letting it stall going into first, her confidence picked up when second caught without much jerking at all.

If only she could cruise like that all day.

She remembered now, the freedom of riding in a nostalgic car like this. Luke's had been slightly newer, but all the same, an eye-turner. Already she had people waving and honking at her as she passed. Made her nervous, but also pretty damn good about being able to drive it.

Bash would be proud.

She turned onto the main road and concentrated on synchronizing her feet to her hand. It was a tricky dance, and somehow Bash made it look easy.

"Great." Red light. Now she was going to look like a dunce trying to take off without jerking the car or squealing the tires.

She revved it up, trying to keep the RPMs at a steady level. But the sound of Bash's car was soon drowned out by the louder, more powerful engine.

A dark cloud in the otherwise clear sky. It consumed her rearview mirror, that menacing hood that held a hungry engine.

Her hands shook, her teeth chattered and her stomach flip flopped. *He thinks I'm Bash.*

The light turned green and she floored it, pulling away for just a little bit. There was no matching driver ability. Of course, she had to remember that the car following her was not from this earth. The people around her probably couldn't even see it like she could.

The nose of the car behind her practically touched the rear bumper, pushing her along while it still revved—like deep, warning growls.

Whimpering, she pressed her right foot down a little farther, switching lanes and blowing a yellow light. Only two more lights and a turn to go.

Then what?

She slowed for the next red light and promptly stalled the car.

Son of a bitch.

"It's okay, Bree. Just get it restarted and ride the clutch a bit more."

Luke's voice. Where was he? She couldn't see him. Was he here? Or was she imagining it?

Why hadn't she insisted Bash come? What was she thinking anyway? "Start, you bastard." Stomping on the gas, she held the clutch down and turned the key. Probably flooding the damn carburetor, but she didn't care.

"No, no. You have to talk sweet to her."

She grumbled something and called it baby. It finally kicked over and she held that gas down until the light turned green.

She was nearly through the intersection when she felt the bump from behind. "Dammit!" Her rearview mirror was black. Completely filled with black. She hit the brakes.

Too late she realized that in her panic, she'd relaxed her left foot and allowed the car to die.

Damn, damn, damn.

"Go, go, go!" Luke's voice tore through her, filled with anger and panic. It translated to her. The gauges blurred, she couldn't remember which gear was which. She felt weight pushing down on her legs. She tried to comply, tried to push that clutch down, but her leg shook from the exertion.

"I can't do this. I can't!" The feeling of utter failure fell over her like a blanket of dread.

"Try!"

She had no doubt now, that Luke stood on the clutch, not her, even though it was her foot on the pedal.

Leaving it in neutral, she felt the 'vette pushing her through the intersection. Horns all around her blared. Her heartbeat nearly drowned the noise out. That and the sound of the starter rotating, but not catching the engine.

The light above her turned yellow. Then red. She was stuck there, in the middle of the intersection.

"Come on!" This was unbelievable.

The roar was upon her before she looked up. The sound of squealing tires, angry horns and one supercharged diesel straining as the driver downshifted in an effort to slow his semi-truck.

Too late.

It hit the passenger side of the Chevy. She saw a bright light, felt the heat, then all went black.

Bree jerked awake with a start.

Shit. Bash's car! Where was he? What had happened?

She reached for the door handle, but when she did, realized that she wasn't in the Chevy anymore. At least Bash's Chevy.

"Oh my God."

She tested her fingers. Touched her face. Pinched her arm. No. It couldn't be. She'd felt it—felt the pain. She couldn't be here, unscathed. Memory of the giant truck bearing down on her. That look of panic in the driver's eyes. Her own scream echoing. Bree closed her eyes and rubbed them.

But when she opened them again, nothing had changed.

She pushed open the door and heard the sirens and yelling voices. She looked behind her. Back at the scene.

This time words weren't even possible.

She slid to her knees, her hands clenched tightly as she screamed. *Please God, tell me this isn't happening.*

Bash was there amidst the wreckage, she picked him out immediately. He threw up his hands and pointed. He was devastated. How she knew from this distance, she couldn't tell, but she knew.

She walked closer. No one seemed to notice her, or else, didn't care if yet one more spectator joined the circle that had surrounded the mangled wreck.

When she saw it, up close, the finality set in.

"No!"

"Poor girl, didn't have a chance," she heard behind her.

"Car stalled, I hear," said another. "Witness said she was having a heck of a time with it. Died right there in the intersection and she couldn't get it started. Semi came around the corner and couldn't stop."

Sobs racked her body. No! No! They couldn't see her. Didn't know she was even there. Bash! Where was he?

"I'm sorry." A hand clamped her shoulder.

She turned. Luke.

He smiled down on her, a sad smile. "Destiny has a funny way of catching us off-guard. I wanted to save you. Rather ironic that I came to make sure Bash didn't alter fate and then realized that it wasn't right. How could it be your time? You were finally learning to live. It seemed so unfair to have it ripped away. But I couldn't help you."

She nodded, her tears unchecked. He took one of her hands and squeezed it. "I need to get back. Bring Bash with you this time, okay? I've missed my buddy."

The man in front of her faded into nothingness. Her hand still tingled where he'd touched her. His words were like adrenaline in her blood. How could she feel that if he were right? How could she be dead and still know hope, and pain, and ache, and regret, and most of all, love?

Bash!

She jumped up and raced over to where he was. Sitting, alone on the curb.

"Bash, it's me. I'm here."

She reached out and touched him, so afraid her hand would float right through his shoulder. That she'd be stuck here, alone, unable to communicate.

But he looked up, that beautiful, strong face lined in horror. She knew that pain, felt it even now. "I'm so sorry," he said. "It wasn't supposed to be like this."

It all made sense to Bash now, the way the car had followed Bree, been visible to her but no one else. And Luke's message. No, he couldn't change the future. Hadn't been able to. But if he would have known, he would have tried with everything he had.

Bree tugged him to his feet and wrapped her arms around his neck. "Can you feel it if I kiss you?" she asked. The fire trucks arrived, pushing everyone back from the site. No one said a word to them.

"Yeah." He felt everything. It was like dying all over again.

She stood on tiptoe and pressed a kiss to his lips. "How come they can't see you?"

"I told you. I'm a ghost."

"I think I am too." She grinned, her teary eyes trying to smile.

He held her tight. It did little good to wish he could turn back time and spare her life. Just as he couldn't go back and spare Luke's.

"No, you don't want to be."

"But I can be with you. There's no reason we can't truly have forever."

She was right. Despite the guilt that had slammed into him the moment of impact, the desperate attempt to save her, she was right. It wasn't because of him. It was her time. Luke had freed him from feeling responsible. *Thank you, pal.*

"Now what?" she said against his chest.

"I don't know."

"Bash. I'm really sorry about your car." Bree stood back with him and watched as the two tow trucks separated the vehicles. There was little left to distinguish his car from a pile of scrap metal. "But…" She grabbed his hand and opened the palm. Into it she dropped a set of keys and closed his hand.

"What's this?" he asked after opening and looking.

Bree smiled and pointed. "How about we take that little hot rod and see if we can't find where that white light leads to."

"Oh, I know where it goes," Bash said, holding Bree tight as they crossed the yellow tape and made their way toward the now silent Corvette. "It leads directly to Hot Rod Heaven."

"Will I still be able to kiss you when we get there?" she asked, looping her arm through his.

"I hope so. Otherwise we'll turn around and drive right back out."

"But we'll need a new car. The 'vette doesn't have a backseat."

Bash tilted his head back and laughed. He loved this woman. Truly loved her. "I'm sure that's not going to stop us."

Enjoy this excerpt from
Dante's Relic
© Copyright Melani Blazer 2004

"It's too late to go back." His words had many meanings.

She shivered.

Dante shifted, then reached down and released the scabbard from his belt and tossed the sword several feet away.

Cammie snagged the opportunity and yanked her wrists apart, easily breaking the single-handed grasp he had on her. She had her hands between their shoulders and pushed up before he could catch his balance and react.

Not that it did her any good. She gritted her teeth and used every muscle she had, but he wasn't going to budge.

And now he was pissed. Quite evident in the way he forcefully breathed out, like a bull flaring his nostrils before charging. She wasn't afraid. If he'd wanted to hurt her, he would have already. Easily would have killed her to take the relic, of that she was sure now.

"What do you want?" she wrenched her arms away despite it being a losing battle.

"Stop fighting me," he hissed. So maybe he wasn't pissed. Hurt. Which meant she did have some impact in him. Good.

"Stop treating me like you're holding me for ransom." Her adrenaline had kicked in when she'd seen that opening. Her body might be tired and she might have resigned herself to staying with him for at least the night, but she didn't have to be pinned to the ground.

"I need to know you won't try to run again. I need you to trust me."

"I won't run, but...trust?" Still, she'd had already handed over the reins of this situation on so many levels.

Instinctively she'd known it was the right thing to do. But that didn't mean she had to like it.

"I've given you my word, I will never hurt you. But there is something out there that will."

She knew that answer—or at least what he was going to say. "This demon."

He shifted his weight slightly. The seriousness of the conversation did little to cool the heat between their bodies. If anything, the fact that he didn't take immediate advantage of her while having her in this compromising position should be added to that "why to trust" column.

He answered, his breath hot on her cheek. "I will never leave you."

Those five words branded her heart.

"But in that...vision. You left me." Her breath caught at the memory of having her soul wrenched from her body. How could she be so inexplicably tied to this man she barely knew?

His whisper echoed in his head. "I didn't leave you. I stepped away to defend you from evil. I'm not going anywhere."

She tried to roll from beneath him, frightened by her own feelings of surrender. Maybe it was another one of those spells he cast over her. However he did that. She was tired. Overloaded. A man who had simply unlocked her pent up emotions and walked in now triggered a sexual awareness. If she didn't get out of his arms, she'd act on it.

They stared at each other for a long moment, as if both contemplating the way she'd lifted her hips to squirm from beneath him. The mere motion alone had triggered some carnal thoughts to form in her mind and she was reminded of the electric current that had passed between them when he'd so carefully freed her hair.

"Are you going to let me up?" she asked him, squinting to see past the shadows and decipher his features. The darkness was too thick, a mask that increased his mystique and played with her common sense.

His breathing increased. "I rather like you here."

"Why?" she said, and half-heartedly tugged at her hands, which he still held above her head.

Instead of answering, he lowered his head. His lips met hers with a force that knocked the breath away from her and left her limp in the grass, as if he'd drawn every last bit of willpower out of her. His mouth opened over her bottom lip and nipped at it, then before she could even sigh, covered her lips again.

Her body betrayed her. She slid her tongue between his lips as he had done to her. All the nerve cells in her body came alive with his groan and increased pressure of his hips against her. As if her surrender to his kiss increased his excitement.

But it was so much more than a kiss.

About the author:

Melani Blazer's mom swears she was born reading, and by age six, was writing little rhymes. It was something she did for fun—even through high school where she was a writer and the copy editor for the school newspaper. But then practical thinking took over and her college focus aimed at science.

Now, too-many-years-to-admit later, she's rediscovered her childhood escape and taken it a step further. She's written stories in a diverse number of genres, but found her true love in paranormals.

To keep her feet grounded in real life, she keeps house with her wonderful husband of 14 years, an almost-teenage daughter, and her cats.

Melani welcomes mail from readers. You can write to her c/o Ellora's Cave Publishing at 1056 Home Avenue, Akron OH 44310-3502.

Why an electronic book?

We live in the Information Age—an exciting time in the history of human civilization in which technology rules supreme and continues to progress in leaps and bounds every minute of every hour of every day. For a multitude of reasons, more and more avid literary fans are opting to purchase e-books instead of paperbacks. The question to those not yet initiated to the world of electronic reading is simply: *why?*

1. *Price.* An electronic title at Ellora's Cave Publishing and Cerridwen Press runs anywhere from 40-75% less than the cover price of the <u>exact same title</u> in paperback format. Why? Cold mathematics. It is less expensive to publish an e-book than it is to publish a paperback, so the savings are passed along to the consumer.

2. *Space.* Running out of room to house your paperback books? That is one worry you will never have with electronic novels. For a low one-time cost, you can purchase a handheld computer designed specifically for e-reading purposes. Many e-readers are larger than the average handheld, giving you plenty of screen room. Better yet, hundreds of titles can be stored within your new library—a single microchip. (Please note that Ellora's Cave and Cerridwen Press does not endorse any specific brands. You can check our website   at   www.ellorascave.com   or

www.cerridwenpress.com   for   customer
recommendations we make available to new
consumers.)

3. *Mobility.* Because your new library now consists of
    only a microchip, your entire cache of books can be
    taken with you wherever you go.

4. *Personal preferences are accounted for.* Are the words you
    are currently reading too small? Too large?
    Too...**ANNOYING**? Paperback books cannot be
    modified according to personal preferences, but e-
    books can.

5. *Instant gratification.* Is it the middle of the night and all
    the bookstores are closed? Are you tired of waiting
    days—sometimes weeks—for online and offline
    bookstores to ship the novels you bought? Ellora's
    Cave Publishing sells instantaneous downloads 24
    hours a day, 7 days a week, 365 days a year. Our e-
    book delivery system is 100% automated, meaning
    your order is filled as soon as you pay for it.

Those are a few of the top reasons why electronic
novels are displacing paperbacks for many an avid reader.
As always, Ellora's Cave and Cerridwen Press welcomes
your questions and comments. We invite you to email us
at service@ellorascave.com, service@cerridwenpress.com
or write to us directly at: 1056 Home Ave. Akron OH
44310-3502.

Discover for yourself why readers can't get enough of the multiple award-winning publisher Ellora's Cave. Whether you prefer e-books or paperbacks, be sure to visit EC on the web at www.ellorascave.com for an erotic reading experience that will leave you breathless.

www.ellorascave.com